THE
MIDNIGHT
LIBRARY

—

VOICES

LOOKING FOR DAYLIGHT? KEEP DREAMING.

THE MIDNIGHT LIBRARY CONTINUES....

VOICES

BLOOD AND SAND

END GAME

THE CAT LADY

THE
MIDNIGHT
LIBRARY

—

VOICES

DAMIEN GRAVES

SCHOLASTIC INC.
New York   Toronto   London   Auckland   Sydney
Mexico City   New Delhi   Hong Kong   Buenos Aires

SPECIAL THANKS TO SHAUN HUTSON

—

ISBN 0-439-86356-2

Series created by Working Partners Ltd.
Text copyright © 2005 by Working Partners Ltd.
Interior illustrations © 2005 by David McDougall

12 11 10 9 8 7 6 5 4 3 2 1   6 7 8 9 10 11/0

Printed in the U.S.A.
First printing, September 2006

Welcome, reader.

My name is Damien Graves,
curator of that secret
institution:

The Midnight Library.

Where is The Midnight Library, you ask?
Why have you never heard of it?
For the sake of your own safety, these questions are better left
unanswered. However . . . as long as you promise not to reveal
where you heard the following (no matter who or *what*
demands it of you), I will reveal what I
keep here in my ancient vaults.
After many years of searching,
I have gathered the most terrifying
collection of stories known to
humanity. They will chill you to
your very core, and make
the flesh creep on your young,
brittle bones. So go ahead, brave
soul. Turn the page. After all, what's
the worst that could happen. . . ?

Damien Graves

THE
MIDNIGHT LIBRARY:
VOLUME I

Stories by Shaun Hutson

—

CONTENTS

VOICES

The hospital corridor seemed to stretch away into forever as Kate Openshaw and her dad walked slowly along it, their footsteps echoing around them. They had walked this walk more times than Kate cared to remember in the three months since her mom had become mysteriously ill.

Outside, the rain was pelting against the large windows that overlooked the hospital grounds. Kate shivered.

"Dad," she said, unable to bear the silence any longer. "How many more tests will they have to do on Mom?"

"I don't know, Kate," her dad replied quietly. "They'll just keep doing them until they find out what's wrong."

"But they've been doing tests for *months* now," Kate protested. "And they still haven't found anything. Not even when they did that big operation on her throat last week."

"I know." Kate's dad slipped a comforting arm around her shoulder. "But we've got to trust the doctors. They're doing their best."

There was a large set of double doors ahead. Kate pushed them hard in frustration. They swung back on their hinges, and she and her dad passed through into the next stretch of corridor. To Kate, it felt as if the pale walls were somehow closing in, growing more and more narrow. "I hate this place," she said as they continued their endless trek.

"No one likes hospitals, Kate," her dad said gently. "But you know we had no choice about coming here. Maybe when the doctors have finished the latest set of tests, they'll have a better idea of what to do."

Kate wasn't sure whether he was trying to reassure her or himself. Probably a little of both.

The rain was falling even more heavily, whipped by

an increasingly strong wind that caused some of the bushes close to the windows to slap their leaves and branches loudly against the glass.

Another set of doors loomed ahead. The sign above them read WARD 6. Kate swallowed hard. That was her mom's ward.

She followed her dad through the doors. A few nurses and patients waved to them. Kate waved back. Everyone on the ward was so friendly and had been ever since her mom had first arrived there.

Kate knew she shouldn't be afraid of coming here, but she couldn't help herself. She glanced at the curtains that were drawn around one of the beds to her right and wondered what was going on behind them. Then she decided she would rather not know.

"You OK?" her dad asked as they approached the two beds at the end of the ward.

Kate nodded.

One of the beds was empty.

The other one was occupied by Kate's mom.

There were two doctors and a nurse standing around the bed. Kate saw that they were all looking very serious.

The older doctor, who Kate knew was called Dr. Venner and was in charge of her mom's case, looked up. Seeing Kate and her dad, he walked over to meet them.

"Has there been a change in my wife's condition, Doctor?" Kate's dad asked anxiously.

"I'm very sorry to say that your wife's condition has worsened, Mr. Openshaw," Dr. Venner replied quietly.

Kate felt a shiver run through her when she heard the words.

"In all my years as a doctor, I've never seen a case like Mrs. Openshaw's before," Dr. Venner went on. "We've tried everything." He put a sympathetic hand on Kate's shoulder. "We'll keep trying, but I can't promise anything, I'm afraid," he said gently.

Kate felt tears welling up in her eyes.

"We'll leave you alone to have some time with her," Dr. Venner finished. He beckoned to the other doctor and the nurse, and the three of them walked slowly away, heads bowed, deep in discussion.

Kate waved at her mom and smiled as bravely as she could. Then she walked over, leaned forward, and kissed her mom's cheek. "How are you feeling, Mom?"

Kate asked, looking at the thick gauze that still covered her mom's throat.

Kate saw her mom's lips move and leaned in closely, as she'd been forced to do since the illness had reduced her mom's voice to a whisper.

"I'm fine, darling," her mom croaked.

But Kate could see that wasn't true. It wasn't true at all.

Kate's dad sat down at the other side of the bed, looking anxious.

Her mom reached up and squeezed his hand before turning her attention back to Kate. "How are you, darling?" she asked. "How's school? What did you do today?" She gasped, as if the effort of speaking was now even more painful.

"Just the usual stuff, Mom," Kate replied, holding her mom's hand tightly.

Just then, another doctor came over. Kate could see the man's ID pinned to his long white coat. DR. GREGORY SOLOMON.

Dr. Solomon gazed at the chart hanging at the bottom of the bed, occasionally making a mark with the pen he'd taken from his pocket. Looking even more serious, he asked Kate's dad to come and chat with him in his office.

Kate watched as her dad disappeared through a door halfway down the ward. Then she felt her mom's hand take her own to get her attention. She leaned in closer so that her mom could whisper in her ear.

"Darling, will you do something for me?" her mom said, again having to force the words out in a gasp.

"Of course, Mom," Kate replied. "Anything!"

Her mom smiled. It was a sad smile. She lifted her head from the pillow to give Kate a kiss, her lips brushing against Kate's ear. Then she gave a long sigh. "It would have been Grandma's birthday tomorrow," she said. "Could you get some flowers and put them on her grave for me?"

"Sure, Mom."

"Take the money from my purse in the locker by my bed," her mom said. "Get a bouquet of irises if you can. Your grandmother loved those."

"OK, Mom," Kate agreed. "I can get them from the florist in the hospital on our way home and take them to the graveyard on my way to school in the morning."

"Good idea," her mom gasped. "I'd rather you did that than go to the graveyard after school. It gets dark early and I don't want you wandering around on your own."

As she moved back slightly, Kate saw that her mom's eyes held an urgent expression. "Don't worry, Mom. I usually walk home with Susie," Kate reassured her.

Then she looked up to see her dad returning from Dr. Solomon's office. He looked pale and defeated.

"I love you, Mom," Kate said, fighting back the tears.

"I love you, too," her mom said, squeezing her hand. "That's why I'm determined to get better. I don't want to leave you and your dad."

"Come on, Kate," her dad said. "We'd better go and let Mom get some rest."

Kate kissed her mom and walked back down the ward. She turned and waved, and her mom smiled weakly back.

As she'd promised, Kate visited the florist near the main entrance of the hospital and bought a bunch of irises, and then she and her dad hurried through the rain to the car.

Kate glanced over her shoulder at the hospital as

they drove away, the rain still hammering against the windshield.

Somewhere in the distance, there was a low rumble of thunder.

By the following morning, the rain had stopped. Despite a sharp chill in the air, the sun shone brightly, reflecting in the puddles that Kate skirted as she walked along the road that led to the church. The air smelled beautifully fresh and crisp. Early morning dew sparkled on spiderwebs like diamonds on thin silver chains.

The streets were still relatively quiet; Kate had left earlier than usual, so that she could visit Grandma's grave before school. She looked down at the bouquet of irises she'd bought the night before.

Ahead of her, the church steeple thrust upward toward the clear blue morning sky. Her footsteps crunched on the gravel path as she made her way through the churchyard entrance and along one of the pathways to the area of the graveyard where her grandmother was buried.

Many of the gravestones near the church were extremely old, and Kate slowed down to glance at the inscriptions. Some of them were hard to read, the letters worn away by the passage of time. A couple of the oldest-looking stones were so blackened by mildew and mold, they looked like rotting teeth sticking up from the ground.

Kate moved closer to wipe away some of the mold, so that she could read the lettering. As she did so, a fat black slug slid into view on top of the gravestone. Kate wrinkled her nose and quickly drew her hand away. She watched the slug glide slowly down the stonework on its sparkling silver slime trail until it disappeared into the wet grass at the base of the stone.

"You won't find any names on those two headstones."

The voice startled her and she spun around quickly, standing up.

It was the minister — Reverend Dodds, who had performed Grandma's funeral a few months ago. His clerical collar stood out with brilliant whiteness against the blackness of his clothes.

"Sorry if I startled you," he said gently.

"It's OK," Kate replied.

The minister narrowed his eyes slightly, then smiled

at her. "You're Kate Openshaw, correct?" he said. "We met at your grandmother's funeral."

Kate smiled and nodded. "That's why I'm here," she told him. "It would have been Grandma's birthday today. My mom asked me to put these on her grave." Kate held up the bouquet of irises.

"What a lovely gesture," said Reverend Dodds. "I won't keep you, in that case."

Kate was about to continue on her way, but then paused and looked back at the two cracked and moldy headstones she'd been inspecting before Reverend Dodds appeared. "You said I wouldn't find any names on these two gravestones," she said. "Why not? I know they're very old but . . ."

"It wasn't the weather or the time that caused the damage to the stones. It was other people," replied Reverend Dodds.

Kate looked up at him, puzzled.

Reverend Dodds grinned. "You'll have to forgive me, Kate, but I can be quite a bore on this subject. I've been studying the history of this church since I arrived here a few years ago. Those two graves are more than three hundred years old. They belong to a mother and daughter who were believed by some parishioners to be witches. The minister at the time dismissed these claims and allowed the women to be buried here in the churchyard. But the parishioners who disagreed with him scratched the women's names from their headstones."

Kate shivered. "Those poor women. I'm on the minister's side. I don't believe in witches."

"Not even the broomstick-riding kind?" Reverend Dodds asked, smiling.

Kate grinned back and shook her head.

"Many of those accused of witchcraft were executed in those days, you know," Reverend Dodds continued. "It was often because they seemed able to foresee the future. Those who executed them said they'd been given the power by the devil, so must be witches."

"It doesn't seem to be such a bad thing to be able to tell the future," Kate remarked. "You'd know about things before they happened. Like which numbers would win the lottery!"

Reverend Dodds smiled. "Well, in times gone by, that kind of ability would have gotten you burned at the stake as a witch." He looked down at the two ancient, weathered gravestones, his tone darkening a little. "Anyone who lived alone, who wasn't liked by others, or who was a little unusual, they were all likely to be accused of being a witch. No one was safe."

Kate nodded.

"Anyway, I'll leave you alone now," Reverend Dodds said, and he turned to walk back toward the church.

Kate watched him disappear inside, then walked briskly along the gravel path to her grandmother's grave.

"Hello, Grandma," she said softly, kneeling beside the headstone. "Happy birthday." She wiped some fallen leaves from the base of the marble headstone and laid the bouquet of irises there. "I brought these for you, from me and Mom. I know they were your favorites." Somehow, it seemed natural to be speaking to Grandma like this. "Mom can't come herself since she's still in the hospital, Grandma," Kate said. "The doctors still can't find out what's wrong with her. I hope that you're watching her, keeping her safe. Wherever you are, Grandma, I hope you're listening and that you're OK."

"I'm fine. Thanks, darling."

Kate spun around, looking for the voice that had whispered into her ear — so close she could have sworn she felt the breath.

The graveyard was still empty apart from herself.

She looked back down at her grandmother's gravestone and swallowed hard. "Grandma?" she said uncertainly. "Grandma, is that you?"

A slight breeze ruffled the hair around the back of her neck. It felt like the soft touch of a hand.

Kate looked around again, but there was no one to be seen. The skin on her arms rose into goose bumps. The delicate bouquet of irises shivered in the wind.

She rose to her feet and then backed away, almost stumbling on to the path.

"Oh, I wish I'd been able to be there! Describe it to me."

"Well, as Aunt Magdalena requested, everyone was wearing purple and white. And you should have seen the way they'd made those flowers spell out her name. It was beautiful. They'd really honored her right."

Again Kate looked around. No one could be seen. Where were these voices coming from? Her heart was thudding against her ribs now.

Kate hurriedly made her way toward the church

gate. As she passed the church, the voices seemed to grow louder.

"It was absolutely beautiful. It really was the most beautiful funeral I've ever been to. Just what Aunt Magdalena would have wanted. . . ."

Kate sighed to herself in relief. A funeral service must have started inside. The church was old. Its ceiling was high. The sound of voices in there would carry.

Kate nodded to herself. That must be it. Mystery solved.

She headed on toward the gate.

"I'm sure Aunt Magdalena would have been watching. She'd have been looking down on it all and smiling."

"Especially when she heard her favorite hymn being played at the end. She always loved the sound of that old organ. . . ."

The voices were growing fainter again.

Kate left the churchyard and hurried on down the road toward school, a cold breeze whipping her hair around her face.

That school day passed the same as every other: a few laughs with Susie and her other friends, a couple of arguments with some of the boys in her class. Talk of what they'd watched on TV the night before. What they were going to do over the weekend.

The only downside had been Daisy Barton, as usual — who had told Susie she had a spare Screaming Monkeys CD that Susie could buy for half-price. The Screaming Monkeys were everyone's favorite band at the moment, and this was the only one of their CDs that Susie didn't have.

"She never told me it had a big scratch on it," Susie complained as the two girls sat at the back of the class. "I didn't realize until after I'd paid her for it and tried to play it at home last night. And she wouldn't take it back. She's always doing things like that to people."

"Daisy only cares about herself," Kate replied. "And she's probably jealous that you managed to get a ticket for The Screaming Monkeys' concert and she didn't because she was too lazy to go to the box office and stand on line for hours like we did."

Susie smiled. "You're probably right," she said, looking more cheerful.

"I've got to go shopping on the way home," Susie told Kate when the final bell rang. "Do you want to come?"

"I'd better get home," Kate replied. "I usually make my father a cup of tea before we go see Mom in the hospital."

"OK, give your mom my love, Kate," Susie said, and she rushed off in the opposite direction.

Kate stood alone for a moment, then set off in the direction of home. It was getting dark already as she passed the church.

"Tell him I want those photos by Friday or I'm not paying."

Kate slowed her pace, the voice loud in her ear.

"I've told him, but he says there's nothing he can do about it."

The tone of the argument was growing more heated. Kate found herself wandering closer to the open church door.

"I'm not going to tell you again. I want them Friday, or I'm not paying."

She poked her head around to see what was going on.

The church was empty.

"Do what you like. I've spoken to him and that's all I can do."

Confused, Kate couldn't figure out where the words were coming from. She took a couple of steps inside the building, glancing at the beautifully colored stained-glass windows.

"Hello, Kate."

She spun around, startled — but this time it was a familiar voice.

Reverend Dodds was standing close behind the door, pinning something to the bulletin board there. "Sorry if I made you jump," he said cheerfully. "May I help you?"

"I heard someone talking," Kate said falteringly. "In here."

"Not unless you heard me talking to myself." He smiled. "And I hope you didn't. They say that's the first sign of madness, don't they?"

Kate nodded, looking around the church again, the other voices still echoing inside her head. She was sure that the argument had come from inside the church. "Sorry to have disturbed you," she said. Then she turned and quickly left.

Kate sat beside her mom's bed. She couldn't stop smiling. Her mom was sitting up, looking better than Kate had seen her for months.

Dr. Venner glanced at the chart he held and shook his head, a smile playing on his lips. "I have to say, your mom is a constant puzzle to us, Kate," he began. "First she comes into the hospital and we can't find out what's wrong with her, and then she suddenly begins to recover and we don't know why. I must say, the improvement is remarkable."

"Does that mean she can come home?" Kate asked.

"Hopefully," Dr. Venner said. "But let's just see what happens, OK? You want your mom back to her old self, don't you? And we certainly don't want her leaving here until she is."

He replaced the chart, smiled at them all, and turned in the direction of another patient farther down the ward.

"Happier now?" Kate's dad asked her.

Kate nodded and smiled. "Do you really feel better, Mom?" she asked.

"Much better," her mom said quietly, reaching out to squeeze Kate's hand.

"It's weird that they didn't know what was wrong with you and now they don't even know what's made you better, but I don't care — all that matters is that you'll be coming home soon," Kate beamed. "I can't wait."

"Your mom's still got to take it easy," her dad told her. "If she became ill without warning, then it might happen again."

"No, it won't," Kate's mom said softly.

"But if you don't know what put you in here, darling," said Kate's dad, "how can you be so sure?"

"I just know," Kate's mom replied. "Anyway, you two will keep your eyes on me, won't you?"

"I'll do whatever you want, Mom," Kate said.

"Even your homework?" her mom said with a smile.

Kate nodded and laughed.

"I got better because of you, Kate," her mom told her, touching her cheek. "You always cheer me up when you visit me. You and your dad." She leaned forward and kissed Kate. "Thank you."

Kate hugged her mom.

"I'm sorry," her mom whispered, looking a little upset.

"What for?" Kate asked, surprised.

"For all the trouble I've caused. All the worry . . ." her mom replied.

"But everything's going to be fine now, Mom, isn't it?" Kate said.

Her mom smiled but didn't answer.

"What are you thinking about, Kate?" Susie asked at school the following day. "You've hardly said a word all lunchtime," she added, putting another potato chip into her mouth. "Is it your mom?"

Kate shook her head. Staring out across the playground, she bit into her sandwich and chewed thoughtfully. "I know this is going to sound stupid," she said, "but have you ever heard voices?"

"What kind of voices?" Susie asked.

"You know, *voices* — when there doesn't seem to be anyone there."

Susie looked thoughtful. "Well, I read in one of my brother's science magazines that alien waves could be picked up by fillings in teeth," she told Kate.

"Alien waves? What are they?" Kate asked.

"Well, the sounds from flying saucers I suppose, from spaceships. I'm not sure I believe it," Susie replied, shrugging. "Seems a little far-fetched that aliens can contact people by using their fillings. But it supposedly has something to do with the metal fillings being a conductor or something — like a radio," she finished. Then her eyes widened. "Why? Have *you* been hearing voices?"

"Yes . . . well, I don't know. I'm probably imagining it. But I'm sure it wasn't aliens," Kate said, smiling. "These were real voices. People having conversations."

"It *could* have been aliens," Susie insisted. "I mean, they might look just like us. *You* might be one, for all I know."

Kate grinned. "If people can pick up alien waves with their fillings," she said, "do you think your brother could pick up a radio station on his braces?"

Both of them collapsed with laughter.

As she neared the church on her way home, Kate felt tense, wondering whether she'd hear voices again. Or was she really just imagining all this?

"I'll see you about six, then, after you've dropped off the kids."

"That's right. Twelve red roses, to be delivered to Ms. B. Burkeman. Thank you."

"Don't forget to pick up some dog food on your way home."

Kate closed her eyes. It had started again. All different voices — seemingly unrelated.

"What time does the film start? We don't want to be late."

"Tell her I'll wear that black dress. I don't want to show up in the same outfit as Kelly."

The voices were raining in on her like missiles.

Feeling panicked now, Kate opened her eyes again, wanting to run, escape from the noise. And then she saw it. A shiny plaque, attached to the church wall near the entrance.

ROOF OF CHURCH
RESTORED BY NATIONAL TELECOM

She looked up. Perched high on the steeple of the church, like a metallic beacon, was an enormous cell phone antenna.

"Yes, it's lovely, isn't it, the new roof?"

At first, Kate thought it was another one of the voices in her head. And then she felt a touch on her arm.

"Are you all right, dear?" came the voice.

Kate turned to see a kind-faced old lady staring at

her, looking concerned. Kate nodded dumbly, unable to explain what was happening to her.

The old lady smiled and pointed to the roof. "They paid for it," she continued. "They did it in exchange for Reverend Dodds allowing them to put the cell phone tower-thingy up there, you see." She studied Kate's features for a moment and shook her head. "Are you sure you're all right, dear? You look awfully pale."

Kate nodded again, and then hurried away, her mind reeling. As she did so, the voices began to lessen.

She stepped back toward the church again.

"I'm telling you, they should have had at least two more goals before halftime. . . ."

"You have reached the voicemail of National Telecom cell phone number . . ."

"Oh . . . hello . . . this cell phone I bought. I'd like to exchange it."

That was the answer. It had to be.

Kate wasn't going mad. The voices she'd heard, the snippets of conversation, they were being relayed backward and forward on cell phones.

And somehow, Kate was picking up conversations from the cell phone antenna.

—

"**M**om, you look so much better," Kate said happily, looking at her mom, who was sitting up in bed. She had a couple of pillows propping her up and much of the healthy color she used to have had returned to her cheeks.

"I *feel* much better, Kate," her mom told her, sipping a cup of tea. "But how do *you* feel, darling?" she asked Kate.

"I'm fine." Kate shrugged. For a moment, she wondered whether to mention the voices, but it seemed selfish. Her mom needed all her strength to get better. The last thing she needed was to worry about Kate.

"Are you sure?" her mom persisted. "Everything all right at school? Susie all right?"

"Mom, I told you. Everything is fine. Why do you keep asking?"

"I'm concerned. You've had a lot of responsibility since I went into the hospital. It hasn't been easy for you. I know that. I'm sorry."

"You keep saying sorry, Mom. It's not your fault you got sick," Kate said.

Her mom shook her head slowly. "You know I love you, don't you, Kate?" she said.

"Mom," Kate said, blushing.

"Just remember, I'll always be there for you," her mom said quietly.

"*A taxi at eleven thirty — yes, I've got that.*"

"*Get out of here and don't come back.*"

Kate opened her eyes and turned over in bed so fast that she nearly fell out. *Not again! Not in my house! How is this happening?* she thought desperately. She put her hands to her ears in frustration, wanting the voices to stop. Somehow, she was now picking up cell phone conversations even when she wasn't close to an antenna.

She stared at the ceiling, but it was a long time before she drifted off into an exhausted sleep.

She awoke with a start the following morning. Sitting up in bed, Kate cautiously touched her ears. She yawned — and could hear herself clearly. No competing voices drowned out the sound.

Kate felt a little more at ease as she washed and dressed.

"Sorry, baby — I'm going to be late — traffic's awful!"

Kate swallowed hard. *Please don't let it be starting again!* she thought.

"Oh, let's go to the Italian place — I feel like spaghetti tonight. . . ."

Kate waited a while, listening to the snippets of conversation passing through. The babbling inside her head seemed to have settled to a manageable level now. How it got there was another matter, though.

Her dad was finishing his breakfast hurriedly when she wandered into the kitchen, the voices still buzzing inside her head.

Kate wondered about confiding in him.

"I've got to go, sweetheart," he said, rushing past her. "Or I'll be late for work." He stopped, turned back, and kissed the top of her head, then disappeared out of the front door. "Love you!"

"Love you, too, Dad." Kate sighed, listening to the sound of his car starting outside.

She quickly ate a bowl of cornflakes and then set off for school.

Kate approached the church nervously. But now

that the phone conversations were reaching her just as easily away from the antenna, nothing much changed as she drew near.

There were several cars parked outside. A funeral was taking place.

Kate could now hear church music mixing with the voices — somebody was playing the organ. She remembered overhearing someone in the church mention the organ. They'd been talking about the funeral of a lady with an unusual name. What was it again? Magdalena something or other. And she'd wanted everyone to wear purple and white.

Kate paused, looking up at the cell phone antenna on the church roof, wondering what she should do about the snippets of conversation that still mingled with the mournful music inside her head.

The melody came to an end and Kate saw six men dressed in black emerge from the church carrying a coffin on their shoulders. Each of them wore tall top hats, with purple ribbons wound around them. They fluttered in the breeze like flags of mourning. The congregation followed — all dressed in purple and white.

As the coffin was turned, she saw that the purple and white flowers adorning the coffin lid formed a name.

MAGDALENA

Kate didn't wait to see any more. She turned and walked hurriedly down the street. She wanted to cry out. To plead with the voices to get out of her head. She wanted to ignore the even more scary thing that had just become obvious to her: Some of the conversations she was hearing hadn't even happened yet! She'd heard Magdalena's funeral *days* ago. But it had taken place this morning.

What did Reverend Dodds call it? Kate thought. *Witchcraft? But I'm not a witch!*

The garbage collectors were making their rounds, emptying cans into the back of their slowly moving truck. The noise of the truck's crusher as it chewed up the trash was deafening. Louder even than the voices inside Kate's head.

"Kate."

She kept walking.

"Kate."

The voice grew louder than the others, and Kate

realized it was coming not from within her skull but from just behind her.

She turned to see Susie scurrying across the street toward her.

"I thought you were ignoring me," Susie said, catching her breath.

"I didn't hear you," Kate told her friend.

"I'm not surprised, with the racket from the garbage collectors," Susie replied. "But I'll tell you someone else who'll be making a racket today: Mrs. Lawson."

"Why?" Kate asked.

"Because hardly anyone will have understood that math homework she gave us. I mean, I know she's a bit of a slave driver but even *she's* never given us anything that hard before. Please don't tell me you thought it was easy."

"Oh, Susie. I haven't even looked at it," Kate said.

"Oops . . ." Susie said. "Any other teacher would probably let you off, what with your mom being in the hospital and all — but not Mrs. Lawson."

Kate sucked in a deep breath. "What am I going to do?" she murmured.

"Er . . . leave the country? Have plastic surgery so she doesn't recognize you?" Susie suggested. "Sorry, there's no point copying mine — I know it's wrong, so she's bound to guess one of us has copied if we both have all the same wrong answers."

"I'll do the homework after homeroom," Kate decided.

"It took me two hours to do one little part of it," said Susie. "And there's two whole pages of questions to work on. You'll never do that after homeroom."

As they entered the playground, Susie went on and on, worrying about the math homework. "I mean," she continued, "how can she expect us to do all that in one night? I bet she never got homework like that when she was in school."

"I'm so sorry, Mr. Byrne. I really do feel quite sick. . . ."

The voice belonged to Mrs. Lawson.

"Since I won't be in class today, I'd appreciate it if you'd tell the class that they can have an extra day to complete the work."

Kate turned to Susie. "Maybe Mrs. Lawson won't be in today," she said as the bell rang.

"Of course she will," Susie protested. "She's never

out. She never gets sick. She's like some kind of alien; she never even gets colds."

Kate looked at Susie and, for a second, considered telling her friend that she'd just picked up Mrs. Lawson's telephone call in her head. Then she thought better of it.

Kate walked over to Daisy Barton. "Daisy," she said.

Daisy Barton turned. "What do you want?" she asked.

"Did you do the math homework?" Kate asked.

"Of course I did," Daisy replied sniffily. "Why? Didn't you?"

Kate shook her head. "But listen, I'll make a deal with you. If Mrs. Lawson is out sick, then Susie and I get to copy your answers, OK? If she's not, then you can have my Screaming Monkeys concert ticket."

Daisy looked at her in shock, and then a smile crept across her face. "Deal," she said. "You must be really scared of Mrs. Lawson, that's all I can say!"

"Kate — what are you doing?" Susie whispered. "You'd better be right."

"I will be," Kate said confidently.

"And if you're wrong?" Susie whispered worriedly.

"I don't think I will be," Kate whispered back.

"Well, we'll know soon if you're right," Susie said. "We have math first."

After homeroom, the class all waited anxiously for Mrs. Lawson to arrive.

But the door opened to let in Mr. Byrne, the principal, instead. He nodded a greeting. "I'm sorry to tell you that Mrs. Lawson isn't feeling very well today," he informed them. "She's just called me on her cell phone to say she was on her way to school, but went back home and won't be coming in."

Someone at the back of the class cheered.

Daisy's jaw dropped, her lips opening and closing like a goldfish.

Kate let out a sigh that was a mixture of relief and delight and glanced sideways at Susie, who shrugged and mouthed silently at her, "How did you know?"

"Mrs. Lawson told me that she gave you all some homework," Mr. Byrne continued. "And she asked me to tell you that you can use this period and until she returns to complete it."

There was another cheer.

Kate looked at Susie again and smiled.

Susie leaned close to her. "You must be a witch," she whispered, grinning broadly.

At first, Kate thought that she was dreaming.

Then she realized that the words and hysterical voices whirling around inside her head were all too real.

She sucked in a deep breath and tried to focus on what the voices were saying. It was almost like trying to tune in a radio.

"Leaving the band . . . can't believe it . . ."

The words continued to spin through her head.

". . . millions of records . . . sold-out tour . . . The Screaming Monkeys won't be the same without him. . . ."

Kate closed her eyes tightly again for a moment, and one single sentence seemed to glow inside her mind like a flashlight in the dark.

"Nooo! How can Richie do this to us?"

Kate shook her head slightly. Richie — leaving the band? That was *worse* than a nightmare. He was her favorite singer in the world.

She looked across to her nightstand, where her

ticket for The Screaming Monkeys' sold-out show was lying like a trophy.

Swinging herself out of bed, Kate crossed the landing quietly, wincing when one of the floorboards creaked. She waited to see if she'd woken her dad but then, deciding she hadn't, she continued on down the stairs and into the living room and flicked on the light.

The daily newspaper was lying on the sofa. Kate flicked through it quickly.

No mention of Richie leaving the band in there — and surely, Kate reasoned, one of her friends would have mentioned it, would have heard about it by now. Especially Susie. She was obsessed with The Screaming Monkeys — though her favorite band member was Karl. The walls of her room were covered with his posters.

Kate waited a moment, then switched on the TV, hurriedly turning down the volume.

The news came and went with no mention of Richie leaving. She tried two other channels.

Nothing.

She turned off the TV and curled up on the sofa, her heart beating fast. It was clear that Richie hadn't left the band. Not yet.

She thought about the telephone conversation she'd heard taking place at a funeral — when it hadn't even happened yet. And how she'd heard Mrs. Lawson's call to Mr. Byrne before that had happened, too.

If the voices in her head were correct again, then Richie leaving The Screaming Monkeys was still to come.

Kate sat still for a long time before heading back to bed. But it was ages before she could sleep. And not just because of the voices buzzing inside her brain.

When the alarm woke Kate the next morning, she still felt a little groggy from lack of sleep, but as she looked across at her Screaming Monkeys ticket, an idea began to form in her mind.

She put the ticket into the side pocket of her school-bag, then hurried downstairs.

Kate ate her breakfast quickly that morning, and she was out of the door before her dad, who just about managed to say good-bye to her before she hurried off down the street.

"Why have you got your concert ticket with you?" Susie wanted to know when Kate took it out of her bag at school. "You'd better hide it from Daisy Barton — she'll only start moaning again because she was too late to buy one herself."

"Well, she can buy this one if she wants to," Kate told her.

"What?" said Susie, open-mouthed. "I thought you were desperate to see Richie live. I read that The Screaming Monkeys won't be touring again for at least a year."

"Well, if Daisy wants this one, she can buy it," Kate replied. "I'm kind of over The Screaming Monkeys. I'd rather buy my mom a nice present for when she gets out of the hospital."

"Ah, that's really kind — but I can't wait to see Karl in the flesh!" Susie smiled. "I wouldn't sell for a million dollars!"

Kate grinned.

"Well, all right then . . . maybe for a million dollars," chuckled Susie.

They saw Daisy Barton walking across the playground with her friends.

Kate strode straight across to her, the ticket proudly displayed. "You wanted a ticket for The Screaming Monkeys, didn't you, Daisy?" she asked.

Daisy's eyes widened as she saw the ticket. "Is this a joke?" she asked suspiciously. "Trying to make me jealous?"

Kate shook her head. "If you want it, you can buy it off me," she told her. "I don't like the band as much now."

"All right," Daisy said. "I'll go home at lunchtime and get the money."

"Sounds good to me." Kate smiled.

Daisy grabbed her arm. "You'd better not change your mind."

"I won't — I promise," Kate said.

"Cool." Daisy grinned. She and her friends walked off.

"That was easy, wasn't it?" Kate said, looking down at her ticket.

Susie stared at Kate and shook her head. "I know how you could have done it, t

There's no way I'm selling mine. I'd rather die than miss this!"

"I think I'll survive," Kate replied as they walked to their classroom. The voices in her head had stilled to a low buzz. A little like flies around a light. The constant murmur was annoying, but she could put up with it. And by the time she'd collected her money from Daisy that afternoon, her head was pretty clear.

"You could get three or four CDs with that," Susie said enviously. "Or a couple of nice shirts."

Kate pushed the money into her bag. "I told you, I want to get something for my mom as a welcome-home present," she said, looking out the window.

"Do you know when she might be leaving the hospital?" Susie asked.

"Not yet, but soon, I hope," Kate replied. "It'll be great to have her home again."

When Kate arrived home from school, she made herself a sandwich and then wandered into the living room and put on the TV. She switched to one of her favorite music shows.

Kate immediately noticed that there were photos of

The Screaming Monkeys behind the announcer. She reached for the remote and turned up the volume.

"So, the unthinkable has happened. . . ." the announcer said. "In the last hour, Richie has announced he has left The Screaming Monkeys! Hard to believe, I know. He is due to appear shortly at a press conference to talk of his future plans. . . ."

Kate chewed thoughtfully on her sandwich as she watched.

"The band has sold more than twenty million albums worldwide, with Richie as lead singer," the announcer continued. "Their label has said that the forthcoming tour will go ahead as planned — but unfortunately for those Richie fans out there, without him."

The phone rang.

Kate got to her feet and picked it up. "Hello," she said, one eye still on the TV screen.

She recognized the voice at the other end of the line immediately. It was Daisy Barton.

"Kate, I've just heard about Richie leaving The Screaming Monkeys," Daisy told her.

"I know. I just saw it on TV," Kate replied.

"Well, the only reason I wanted to see them was

because I like Richie!" Daisy yelled into the phone. "I don't want to go anymore — I want my money back!"

"Sorry, Daisy," Kate said firmly. "If you don't want to go to the concert anymore, it has nothing to do with me."

Kate hung up and then walked back to the sofa and sat down, gazing at the TV screen. The announcer was still going on about the band.

Kate took another bite of her sandwich and wondered how Daisy Barton was feeling.

"*Listen, I'm not going to put up with much more of this. There has been no heat for two days now and no one's come to fix it.*"

A man's voice. He was angry.

"*Did you see what she looked like in that dress the other night? I told Shana that I wouldn't be caught dead in something like that.*"

A woman's voice this time.

Kate heard the snippets of conversation moving around inside her head. She felt tired, and the low buzzing of the voices was making her feel even more sleepy. She hadn't slept well for the last two nights, and now, seated close to the soothing warmth of the radiator in the classroom, she was having trouble staying awake.

"I know it's sad about her dog dying. She'd had it for ten years. It was like a member of the family, I suppose."

Another woman's voice.

"So, in the Greek myths, most of the characters were either punished or rewarded by the gods. A little like Kate is likely to be punished by me for not listening in class."

Immediately, Kate jerked her head up from her desk to see the face of the teacher staring at her.

"Sorry, Mr. Curtis," Kate said.

"Is the story of Cassandra boring you, Kate?" Mr. Curtis asked.

Several of her classmates were laughing now. Kate felt herself blushing. "No, Mr. Curtis," she said.

"So, Cassandra was given the gift of prophecy by Zeus, king of the gods," Mr. Curtis continued. "She was able to see into the future, but the problem was, no one would believe her prophecies, and more tragically, she was powerless to change what was going to happen."

Kate looked apologetically at Mr. Curtis and tried

to concentrate on the words she heard coming from the front of the class.

"Matt actually likes her. I asked him."

Kate shook her head, trying to ignore the new voice.

"He likes Kate. I'm telling you the truth. I spoke to him after he played soccer yesterday."

Suddenly, Kate didn't want the voice to go away. Matt likes Kate? It could only be Matt Albert. He was the best soccer player in school — and the most popular.

Matt likes Kate.

"Wow," Kate said loudly.

"Something interesting, Kate?" Mr. Curtis asked her pointedly. "Have you found a part of Cassandra's story that's finally grabbed your attention?"

"Sorry, Mr. Curtis," Kate replied, her cheeks turning red.

She dropped her head toward the textbook opened on her desk, as much to mask her delight as anything else. So Matt Albert liked her. . . ? Well, perhaps it was about time she told him that she felt the same way. Wow — she might have her first boyfriend!

Kate glanced at the clock and saw that it was almost lunchtime. She decided she'd go and speak to Matt then. He was always to be found in the same place: kicking a ball around with his friends on the soccer field — usually with three or four girls watching him as they pretended to talk about something else.

The time passed slowly for Kate but, when the bell finally rang, she was the first one out of the classroom.

Kate ate her lunch hurriedly, impatient to get over to the soccer field and wait for an opportunity to talk to Matt.

As she got up to leave, Susie got up, too. "Where are you rushing off to?" she asked curiously.

"I need to do something," Kate told her. "I'll tell you all about it later — won't be long." Then she hurried away, leaving Susie looking puzzled.

Kate forced her way down the crowded school hallway until she reached the exit into the playground. She could see that there was already a group of boys from the next year up, kicking a ball around. As she drew closer, she picked out Matt Albert among them.

Matt likes Kate. She felt a tingle run up her spine.

But the thought of marching across the field in front of all his friends and saying that she liked him, too, was way too embarrassing. Kate decided she'd watch him and his friends playing soccer, and then try to get to talk to him on his own, afterward.

Two of the boys kicking the ball around had already noticed Kate standing there. She smiled at them. Maybe they already knew that their friend Matt liked her.

"Who did you say Matt liked?"

Kate winced, the boy's voice in her ear was so loud. There was a crackling sound like static.

"Kate. But I don't think she knows yet."

Kate recognized the same whispered voice in her head she'd heard in class. She smiled to herself.

"Kate's in the year ahead of him, though. I suppose he likes the fact that she's so athletic. And she does look great in her volleyball uniform."

For a second, Kate was confused. And then she remembered tall, slim, volleyball-playing, blonde Kate Kirby in the year ahead of Matt.

Was *that* who he liked? Not her? Kate went all hot and cold in embarrassment.

"Want to play, Kate?" one of the boys called, kicking the ball toward her.

Matt Albert ran past her after the ball. He didn't even look at her.

Kate felt her face burning red. "I was looking for Susie. I thought I saw her come this way," she lied. And she turned and headed back toward the playground.

"If you want to play, just come back and tell us," one of the other boys shouted.

She heard laughter echoing behind her. But the laughter was nothing compared to the embarrassment she would have felt if she'd gone through with talking to Matt. What a narrow escape! Kate felt almost sick at the thought of how close she had come to making an absolute fool of herself.

The voices had their uses, but it seemed that they could get her into trouble, too, if she wasn't careful!

"That noise is enough to drive anyone crazy," said Susie as she and Kate approached school the following day.

There was a truck parked in the street outside the

apartment building that loomed over the school. Part of the street had been dug up; the eardrum-shattering sound of a drill filled the air.

Kate didn't answer. The loud and abrasive sound of nearby construction meant that she was spared the more intrusive sounds of voices inside her head for a while. She saw two men unloading a large black metal object from the back of the truck.

She realized with horror that it was a cell phone antenna, identical to the one on top of the church steeple. "They're putting that on top of the apartment building?" she gasped in alarm.

"Yes, didn't you hear about it on the local news?" Susie asked. "They're putting them up all over town. Some of the residents are really angry about it."

Kate winced. She'd had a headache from all the snippets of phone conversations coming into her head since she'd woken up that morning. Over the last few days, there had been more and more of them. And no wonder, if cell phone antennas were being put up all over town. But now there was going to be one next to school, too. It would be intolerable!

"Are you all right, Kate?" Susie asked.

Kate shrugged vaguely, her gaze fixed on the top of the high-rise. "I've got a bad headache, that's all. . . ." she said. As they watched, Kate saw the antenna being raised — a black arrowhead against the clouds.

During the history lesson that morning, the hum of voices coming into Kate's head suddenly escalated to a roar, rushing in at her from all directions. The new antenna must have started to work. It felt to Kate as if her brain was a merry-go-round in the center of a busy intersection, words driving at it from everywhere at once. She put a hand to the back of her neck.

"You should see the school nurse if you don't feel any better," Susie whispered.

Kate tried to nod, but the pain was too intense. She feared she would either pass out or simply go crazy right there on the spot.

"You'll have to go to the nurse," Susie insisted.

"You're right," Kate agreed. She didn't really want to go to see Nurse Williams. The extremely sour-faced school nurse was never very sympathetic. But Kate had to do *something*.

She put her hand up to ask their teacher's permission.

Slowly, trying to keep her head as still as possible, Kate approached Nurse Williams's office. She knocked on the door and then walked in.

From the small waiting area, Kate could see Nurse Williams at her desk in the office beyond. She was on the phone. She signaled for Kate to take a seat.

Kate slumped onto the chair and put her hands to her head again. The pain was increasing.

"Hang on a minute," Nurse Williams said. "I've got someone waiting. I'll just see what they want." She put the phone to one side and came out to Kate, eyeing her somewhat suspiciously. "Yes, dear?" she said.

"I've got a really bad headache," Kate told her. "I was wondering if there was something you could give me for it."

The nurse looked at her again, then nodded. "Wait there," she said, and then disappeared back into her office.

Kate saw her pick the phone up again.

"Another one with a headache," Nurse Williams said into the mouthpiece. "Backache. Stomachache. Headache. They use any excuse to get out of class, some of them."

Kate felt like calling over — she *wasn't* using the pain as an excuse. She would have given anything to make it stop. Just as she would have given anything to silence the ever-chattering voices inside her head.

"Always complaining," Nurse Williams continued to her unseen friend. "I'm fed up with it. They're all the same. Anything to get out of school for a couple of hours."

She returned with two white tablets and a glass of water. "Take these," she said sharply. "And then you go straight back to class."

"But I think it might be a migraine," Kate replied, accepting the tablets. "I feel a little sick and dizzy, too."

Nurse Williams rolled her eyes. "So you want to go home, do you?"

"Yes, please," Kate said faintly. "I don't think I could go through the rest of the afternoon like this."

Nurse Williams sighed and called Kate's dad.

He arrived within half an hour.

Kate climbed gratefully into his waiting car and lay back in the passenger seat.

"You look awful, Kate," her dad said worriedly, reaching out to touch her forehead. "Let's get you home. It's lucky I'm on the late shift at the factory tonight, otherwise I wouldn't have been there when the nurse called."

"I just need to lie down, Dad, and try to get rid of this headache," Kate told him.

"I hope you can sleep with all the noise," her dad said.

"What noise?" Kate asked.

"Outside the house. National Telecom are putting up one of those cell phone antennas right across the street."

Kate almost burst into tears. *Not another one*, she thought.

As her dad swung the car onto their street, she saw the National Telecom van parked across the street and the men busily erecting the antenna.

Kate practically fell from the car and her dad hurried around to the passenger side to help her.

"Come on, let's get you inside," he said comfortingly.

Kate's vision swam, and she thought her legs were going to buckle. Her dad supported her as they made their way into the house. The sound from outside dimmed, but the roaring inside Kate's head continued.

Her dad helped her into the living room, and she sat down on the sofa.

He knelt beside her, stroking her forehead. "Trust you to feel bad today of all days," he said, smiling, still gently brushing her hair from her face. "I wanted to give you the good news when you got home."

"What good news?" she asked groggily.

"I spoke to the doctor at the hospital today, and he said that your mom can come home in a couple of days. Whatever was wrong with her has now almost completely cleared up. She still needs time to get back to normal, but she's improving all the time."

Kate gave a weak smile. "Mom starts getting better and I start to feel bad," she joked.

"I spoke to your mom myself on the phone," her dad continued. "It was great to hear her sounding more like her old self. She said she couldn't wait to speak to you. There's something she wants to tell you." He got up. "I'll go and make us a cup of tea, OK? You just lie here and try and get some rest. We'll go and see your mom tonight before I go to work."

Suddenly, Kate felt she just couldn't wait any longer to see her mom again. "No, Dad, I want to see her now," she said, sitting up. She winced at the pain inside her head.

"But you're not well enough, Kate," her dad said, looking concerned.

"I want to see her, Dad. Please . . ." Kate pleaded. "I really miss her when I'm not feeling well." She hesitated. "Dad, I haven't been feeling well for a while now," she confessed. "But I haven't wanted to worry Mom, her being sick herself. Now, though . . . well, I just want to talk to her about it."

Her dad looked at her, then reached out gently and touched her forehead with his hand.

"I understand, Kate. You are so considerate of your mom."

"So can we go and see her now, Dad?"

"Let's go," he smiled. "I'll get my coat."

—

Kate's mom was sitting up, the bandages removed from her throat, her hair done, and her makeup on. She looked like her old self. Healthy and beaming. "Hello, darling," she said to Kate in a clear, if somewhat husky, voice.

Kate rushed over to her mom and hugged her.

"I didn't expect you at this time of the day," said her mom. "You should be at school."

"I had to come home," Kate told her. "I had a terrible headache. I've been getting them for days now. Headaches and —"

Kate's mom placed a hand on one of Kate's. "I bet you haven't been drinking enough water, darling," she said, interrupting. She looked at Kate's dad. "Would you mind going and getting some bottled water from the machine, Harry?" she asked.

"Of course," Kate's dad replied with a smile. "I won't be long."

After he left, Kate's mom turned and gazed at Kate intently. "And what else has been happening to you, Kate?" she asked quietly.

"Phone conversations. Coming into my head. I can hear people talking, Mom," Kate told her. "On cell phones. All the time. And sometimes, the stuff I hear hasn't even happened yet. It's like I hear what's going to happen before it actually does. Like I can hear the future. But I know that's stupid. What's happening to me, Mom? Am I going crazy?"

"No, Kate, you're not." Her mom lowered her gaze slightly and squeezed Kate's hand. "Kate . . ." she continued hesitantly, "I knew this time would come for you and now that it has, you need to know what's happening."

Kate looked warily at her mom.

"You have a gift, Kate," her mom told her. "At least, that's what we call it. Some people might call it a curse, but it can be used wisely so we've always considered it as a good thing."

"Mom, I don't understand," Kate said, feeling a little scared now.

Kate's mom sighed. "It started with your great-great-grandmother Elizabeth," she began. "Elizabeth was celebrating her twelfth birthday. The house where her family lived was right next to a telegraph pole. There was a terrible storm raging, but Elizabeth insisted on trying out her new umbrella. She went out into the garden and, in a freak accident, lightning hit the pole and then forked into Elizabeth." Kate's mom paused for a moment, as if waiting to be sure that Kate was taking in the information.

"At first, everyone thought Elizabeth was dead," Kate's mom continued. "But somehow, she had survived. And she had also been given the gift."

"What *is* the gift, Mom?" Kate asked her impatiently.

"As Elizabeth got older, she developed the ability to overhear telephone conversations — just like you can now," Kate's mom explained. "And when her own daughter turned twelve, it was passed on to her, too. It's been passed on from generation to generation ever since — always from mother to daughter when the daughter turned twelve. And from the time you were born, I knew that you'd have to inherit it one day."

Then she sighed. "But by the time you turned twelve, three months ago, the world had become so filled with telephones, the voices had become almost unbearable. I decided not to inflict the gift on you. I resisted and resisted the urge."

Her eyes filled with tears. "Kate, I think that if I hadn't given in and passed the gift on to you when I did, I would have died."

Kate's eyes widened. *"That's* what made you sick?" she asked incredulously.

Her mom nodded. "But I couldn't tell anyone. Elizabeth confided in two people, and they both collapsed and died."

Kate shook her head, finding it hard to take all this in. "So that's why you began to get better again? Because you passed the gift on to me?" she asked.

Her mom nodded again. "When I kissed your ear . . ." She wiped away a tear that ran down her cheek. "Do you remember? Just before I asked you to buy flowers for Grandma's grave."

Kate nodded, and then hugged her mom. "It's not your fault, Mom."

Kate's mom gave her a watery smile. "Thanks, darling — I was worried that you'd hate me. . . ." She blew her nose. "But you *must* learn how to control it. You have to master the gift, not let it take over your mind. I can help you do that. Grandma knew how dangerous it could be if it was used wrongly. She warned me about it just like I'm warning you now. She was frightened of it toward the end. She heard of her own death. . . ."

"What do you mean?" Kate asked, startled.

Kate's mom squeezed her hand again. "She heard her doctor talking on his phone with the hospital. She knew what was going to happen, but she couldn't stop it. . . . That's why your grandmother and I moved home so many times. We had to."

"I don't understand," Kate said.

"People are always frightened of what they don't understand, darling," Kate's mom said sadly. "Sometimes your grandmother tried to warn others of something that was about to happen — but it would scare them. Grandma was once even called a witch, and they threatened to burn our house down if we didn't leave."

"And I first heard voices in a churchyard where people had been victimized for being thought witches, too," Kate said flatly as she remembered the scratched-out gravestones Reverend Dodds had talked to her about.

"As I said, Kate, people are afraid of things they don't understand. I want you to understand. I want you to let me help you cope with the gift — and use it to help others, even if we must guard against letting them know what we are doing, to protect ourselves."

Kate sat still on the edge of her mom's bed, her head bowed, voices whirling around inside her brain. "*Am* I a witch?" she asked quietly.

Her mom pulled her close and hugged her. "No. You're not a witch," she smiled. "You're not a freak and you're not a monster. You're just . . . special."

"But what if I don't want to be?" Kate asked, her irritation rising. She felt tears stinging her own eyes now.

"Don't be angry, Kate," her mom pleaded. "It won't do any good."

"Cold, refreshing beverages for everyone," Kate's dad said, walking in. He presented three bottles of water arranged neatly on a tray beside three disposable cups.

"I just want to go home," Kate said. "Take me home, Dad, please."

Her dad looked surprised. He looked at Kate, then at her mom. "I thought we were going to have something to drink," he said.

"I'd like to go now, please," Kate insisted. She looked

at her mom. "Unless there's anything else Mom wants to tell me." Then she turned and walked away.

"We'll talk more when I get home, Kate," her mom called. "Everything'll be fine."

Kate wished she could believe that.

It was after midnight. Kate knew that. But how late she had no idea. She didn't bother looking at her watch. All she knew was that she couldn't sleep. The voices were still inside her head but so, too, was the news her mom had given her earlier that evening: the knowledge of why the voices were there and the fact that, as far as Kate knew, they would be there for the rest of her life.

She turned over in an effort to get to sleep, but it was useless.

Her mom's words, the words of other conversations from inside her brain, they all mingled together to form one mass of confusion.

Then, suddenly, a conversation came into her head with such crystal clarity it was as if it was being spoken directly into her ear.

"You'd better be right about this job. I'm not getting caught again. Ten months in prison was enough for me. If anyone gets in the way this time, they'll be sorry."

This voice was low and menacing. Little more than a growl. Kate felt a shiver run down her spine.

"It'll be fine. Trust me. The owners are away for the weekend, the whole family. There's no burglar alarm. We'll be able to break in really easily. He keeps his collection of gold coins in a cabinet in the dining room. It'll be a piece of cake."

This voice was quiet and nervous.

Kate sat up. Susie's dad had a collection of gold coins. And she and her family were away for the weekend. Then she shook her head. It must be a coincidence, surely.

The low, menacing voice cut in again: "Just remember: This job is too big to mess up. If there is anyone inside the house when we go in, then we get rid of them — one way or another. Tell me the address again."

"Twenty-two Arcadia Avenue . . ."

There was a deafening hiss of static in Kate's ear, and she winced. Her heart was thumping. That was Susie's house! It was going to be robbed!

She waited, hoping to hear more of the conversation,

but there was nothing. Instead she picked up two people talking about a movie they'd just watched. She let out a breath of frustration.

What should she do now? Alone in the darkness, Kate realized that she might be able to stop the robbery. Was this what her mom had meant about the gift being used wisely?

She would have to go to the police. She would warn them. They'd be waiting for the criminals; they'd catch them in the act.

Kate nodded to herself. She even managed a smile.

She switched on the light and fumbled for a paper and pencil, writing down as much of the conversation as she could remember.

She'd phone the police and tell them what she knew. Tell them she'd heard a robbery being planned. She didn't have to tell them how she knew. She didn't even have to give them her name. For the first time in what seemed like ages, Kate felt in control.

She crept downstairs and dialed the number of the local police station.

"Police station," a voice said. "May I help you?"

"I want to report a robbery," Kate said.

"Where?" the policeman asked.

"Twenty-two Arcadia Avenue."

"And when did it happen?"

Kate swallowed hard. "Well, it hasn't happened yet. But it is *going* to be robbed."

"Oh, really, when?" the policeman asked.

"Well . . . I don't actually know," Kate replied. "But I've just heard two men talking about it."

"And where did you hear them talking about it?" the policeman asked.

"I was in my bedroom," Kate told him.

There was a pause.

"In your bedroom?" the policeman asked. "The men were in your bedroom?"

"No," Kate replied impatiently. "I heard their telephone conversation — in my head."

Kate heard a sound somewhere between a cough and a groan at the other end of the line.

"Inside your head?" the policeman said slowly. "And where are these men coming from to rob the house at Twenty-two Arcadia Avenue? Mars? Saturn? Jupiter?"

"I did hear them . . . I did!" Kate insisted. "They're going to steal a collection of gold coins!"

The policeman sighed. "So they're going to rob this house, are they? You heard them say so inside your head. You just don't know when they're going to do it?"

"No, I'm sorry, I don't. It could be any time," Kate agreed. "And they said that if anyone got in their way, they would kill them!"

"What is your name, miss?" the policeman asked, sounding more serious now.

Kate hesitated. "I don't want to give my name," she said. "But you've got to believe me."

"You don't want to give your name because you know you'd be in trouble for making this sort of a call," the policeman said. "Now, what is your name?"

"This is going to happen. I swear it," Kate said. "You have to believe me!"

"Well, when it does, you come and let me know. Until then — stop wasting police time."

Kate slammed down the phone in frustration.

She considered calling Susie on her cell to tell her about the conversation she'd overheard, but thought better of it. Susie wouldn't be any more likely to believe the story than the policeman, and Kate wouldn't have blamed her.

Kate hurried back upstairs to her bedroom and got dressed. Then she searched for her digital camera. She checked to see if the camera had batteries in it, then stuffed it into the pocket of her jacket.

If she could get some photos of the robbers, then she could at least show those to the police. They'd have to believe her then.

She went back downstairs and then stepped outside into the cold night and set off in the direction of Susie's house.

It took Kate less than twenty minutes to reach Susie's street. She looked up at the high bushes that formed a natural barrier and shielded the house from prying eyes.

Susie's family home was large, with a big front yard and a driveway that ran for about fifty yards from the road to the front of the double garage next to the house.

There were a number of trees around the front of the house, and Kate thought that one of those might give her the best vantage point to watch from.

She climbed up into the lower branches of one near to the front door, then took the camera from her pocket and peered through the viewfinder. She had a good shot of the driveway and the front door and windows.

Now, all she had to do was wait.

Inside her head, the voices babbled away without stopping.

"Why won't you just shut up?" Kate muttered, banging her forehead with one hand.

Suddenly, she heard two unpleasantly familiar voices inside her head.

"Have you found the girl?"

It was the rasping, gravelly-voiced burglar.

"Not yet."

The other burglar sounded more edgy and nervous than ever.

"Find her. Now."

Kate swayed in shock, her heart beating madly against her ribs. Were they talking about Susie? Had Susie and her family returned home early? Was Susie going to disturb the robbers? Kate had to stop it from happening somehow! But she knew there was no point in calling the police again. If they hadn't believed her the first time they wouldn't believe her now, either.

"Do as I say."

It was getting colder, and Kate's breath clouded in the air every time she exhaled. She was shivering, despite her thick coat and sweater.

She was about to look at her watch when she heard footsteps coming up the driveway.

It was two men, keeping to the shadows as they drew nearer to the house.

Kate could see that one of them was carrying something in his hand that looked heavy. She thought it might be a crowbar.

She reached into her pocket and pulled out the camera, preparing herself.

The men made straight for a side door. They were inside the house within seconds. Kate slid from her perch, landing on the ground, and ran across to hide behind some bushes near the same door. From that position, she could get a clear shot of the men as they came out carrying their stolen goods.

She waited.

And waited.

It seemed as if hours passed but no one came back out of the house. Kate felt her heart thumping harder. What if they'd gone out another way and she'd missed them? She'd have no evidence of the robbery to show the police.

Kate decided to go in.

Just inside the doorway was an open trapdoor. Kate looked down the steep flight of stone steps that led to the cellar.

Perhaps it wasn't such a good idea going down there. But Kate edged slowly downward, step by step. After all — if her best friend was in trouble, she might be the only person who could save her.

She continued to block out the voices in her head as best she could, to concentrate on listening for any movement.

Even though she knew the dangers of her situation, Kate couldn't help taking a moment to stare in amazement at the contents of Susie's dad's cellar. It was a gigantic room that ran the length of the entire house, disappearing into black shadows in all directions. There were packing cases everywhere, some of them open. But there was no sign of the men. Kate went back up the stairs and out into the cold night once more. *The men must have left through the front of the house*, she thought.

And then she spotted the two men making their way back down the driveway.

Kate ducked back behind some bushes and raised her camera, preparing to take some pictures — but she lost her balance and the camera dropped to the ground.

The noise shot through the air like a bullet.

The men turned around and saw Kate.

"Catch her!" the gravelly-voiced robber roared.

Kate had no choice. She ran. She jumped out of the bushes and raced across Susie's lawn, taking off down the street. Footsteps pounded behind her, drawing closer and closer. Her muscles screamed in pain, the cold air sliced across her face, and still she ran. And still he followed.

She would never be able to outrun him, she realized. If she didn't think of something, fast, he would catch her. And then —

Kate made a sharp turn, ducking into a narrow alley

between two rows of houses. She ducked behind a giant brown Dumpster. And she held her breath.

A moment later, a shadowy figure appeared at the opening of the alley. Kate pressed herself against the dank brick wall, and waited.

The man poked his head into the alley and looked around. Then he shrugged his shoulders and pulled out a phone. He was close enough that Kate could hear the dialing of numbers. Close enough that she could hear the tinny voice on the other end of the line.

"Have you found the girl?"

"Not yet," the man replied, leaning slightly against the Dumpster. She squeezed her eyes closed in terror, and hugged her knees.

"Find her," the tinny voice commanded. *"Now."*

Kate heard the phone snap shut. And then she heard the man's thumping footsteps fading away.

She waited a long moment. Then another. Silence.

Kate was halfway home when she lost count of how many antennas she had passed. The voices were there all the time now, strange conversations buzzing in her ears and making her head throb. But it seemed that with every step she took, they grew louder and stronger. And her own voice — her own *thoughts* — had to work harder and harder to battle their way to the surface.

She glanced up. Almost every house on this street had a National Telecom antenna sprouting from its roof.

"And I told him, if he doesn't change his ways, I'm going to walk right out that door!"

"Did you think I should wear the miniskirt tomorrow, or the new pants suit?"

"Did you see him make that play? I've never seen anything like it!"

Kate pressed her hands against her ears, trying to block out the noise. But it was no use. The words rushed in faster and faster, blending together. And then a familiar voice broke through the confusion.

"Are you sure there's nothing you can do for her?" It was her dad. *"I can't bear to lose her, not now."*

Kate stopped short. Was her mother going to get sick again? A sob caught in her throat. She needed her mom — now, more than ever.

"I'm sorry. She's in no physical danger," another voice said. A doctor, Kate realized. It must be. *"We can certainly keep her comfortable indefinitely — but I'm afraid there's nothing else we can do."*

"No physical danger?" her father asked, sounding as desperate as Kate felt. *"But what about her state of mind?"*

"I'm sorry," the doctor said again. *"But I'm afraid you may never get her back the way she was — she may be lost to this madness. Forever."*

Kate couldn't catch her breath. She couldn't stop shaking. But she needed to pull it together, she realized. She needed to get home and warn her parents. Maybe if they got her mom to the hospital quickly, maybe they could fix whatever was wrong with her. Before it was too late.

She wanted to run home, as fast as she could. But as the voices grew louder, it was just so hard to move. So hard to think. They were flooding her brain, crowding out her own thoughts.

"Did you hear what she said to me when —"

"My sink is clogged and I —"

"If you really loved me, you'd —"

Kate sank to her knees, the strength flooding out of

her, as if the voices were washing it away. She was drowning in other people's words.

"I need —"

"I want —"

"If only —"

Kate tried to cry for help, but she couldn't find her voice. She was losing herself — and losing the will to fight.

The voices battered her brain. They beat against her like waves of noise, dragging her under. Dragging her deeper and deeper.

The street was dark and empty. There was no one to hear her scream.

But Kate couldn't scream anymore. Couldn't speak. Couldn't move.

Although she was in no physical danger, the madness was consuming her. . . .

And the voices took over.

A Perfect Fit

Justin Vale brought the ball under control with a single deft touch of his right foot. "That's a superb first touch from Vale!" he called in his best commentator's voice. "He seems to go one way, then —"

Justin moved the ball effortlessly with the outside of his foot, avoiding a lunging tackle from one of his friends. "He got away from the clumsy defender!" Justin shouted triumphantly as his friend went sprawling behind him. "Just the goalie to beat now. Will he go left or right? The goalie doesn't know what to do."

Justin shaped to strike the ball hard, then leaned back slightly and jabbed his toe under it. The kick was

perfect. The ball floated over the prone goalkeeper —
who had gone to ground expecting a low shot — and
into the corner of the net. Justin punched the air with
delight. "Six nothing!" he shouted, beaming. "And the
crowd is on its feet to cheer this incredible new talent,
chanting the name of Justin Vale as he completes his
double hat trick."

He glanced at his best friend, Mark Wells, and
grinned. "It *is* six, isn't it?"

"You should know, you've scored them all,"
laughed Mark.

Justin and his friends always celebrated the end of
the school week with a pickup game in the local park.
Once more, Justin controlled the ball effortlessly, rode
a clumsy challenge from his friend Paul, and played a
perfect pass into Mark's path. The goalkeeper never
stood a chance. The ball flew past him like a rocket,
and Justin and Mark wheeled away in delight. Justin
had never played this well in his life. Every touch was
brilliant, every pass beautifully weighted. Every shot
was of incredible power or delicate brilliance. Even his
speed seemed to have increased.

"I think it's those new sneakers of yours, making you play better," said Mark, slapping Justin on the back. "I wish I had a pair."

Justin smiled and looked down at his feet. Not only did his new sneakers look great, they were also a perfect fit.

Darkness was falling as Justin and Mark said good-bye to the other boys and made their way home.

"Twelve goals in one game," Mark grinned. "That's got to be some kind of record."

Justin was about to answer when the sudden wail of sirens made them both look around.

A fire engine shot past like a huge red bullet, its bright lights spinning. It was followed seconds later by another, both hurtling up the main road and racing around the corner.

"It must be a pretty big fire," Justin murmured, watching the fire engines speed down the busy road.

"It looks like they're heading for the shopping center," added Mark, gazing after the accelerating vehicles.

"Oh, well, nothing to do with us," Justin said.

As Justin reached his house, he glanced at the front yard and smiled. From the look of it, his mom had been gardening all day. Behind the low and perfectly tended privet hedge, a paved path wound across the lawn to the front door. Around its snakelike curves were flower beds, each one now weed-free and stocked with new shrubs and plants. The assorted colors of their blooms were radiant even in the fading light.

Justin walked up the path toward the front door, shaking his head. All that beautiful lawn that he could have played soccer on — wasted on flowers and shrubs. Although, if Justin was honest with himself, he enjoyed having a home with a nice colorful garden. Not that he'd ever have told his tough-guy friends. He could imagine their reaction.

For as long as Justin could remember, his mom had taken great pride in her flower beds — she loved how they made their house stand out from most of the others on the street. And for years now, Justin had been doing something he knew would send his mom into a rage if she ever found out about it.

Flower-bed jumping.

It was like a hobby to him. He'd begun with the smaller beds and graduated to leaping over the larger ones as he'd grown older and bigger. So far, though, clearing the largest bed, just in front of the living-room window, had eluded him.

Justin had nearly made it so many times, but no matter how he varied his preparation, or at what point he started his jump, the result seemed to be the same. His feet would catch the back of the flower bed, trampling the borders that his mom spent so long trimming.

He glanced at the house and then stepped onto the lawn and walked across to one end of the biggest bed. He stood there, glancing at its pristine array of flowers.

Just one more jump.

He braced himself ready, and then hesitated.

No — he couldn't. One misjudgment and he'd wreck all the newly planted flowers. Mom would go completely berserk. And besides, if he landed in the mud, he would dirty his new sneakers and he didn't want that. No. The next jump could wait until another time.

"Justin!"

The sound of his name caused him to spin around.

His mom was at the living-room window. "Justin," she repeated, waving him inside. "Come in — now."

He hurried in, kicking off his new sneakers and leaving them in the hall, and then wandered into the living room.

His mom was staring at the television. "What is it, Mom?" he asked, slumping into the nearest armchair and gazing at the news on TV.

"You know that place where you got your new sneakers?" his mom asked.

"Where I was *awarded* with my new sneakers, Mom," Justin corrected her, "for being Athlete City's ten thousandth customer, remember?"

"Well, you're lucky you got them when you did," his mom told him. "Look."

Justin moved to the edge of his seat, listening to the reporter's commentary as the TV cameras showed the burned-out shell of the large sports store in town.

"The fire, which has destroyed much of the building, is believed to have begun in the early hours of the morning," the reporter

said. *"Police and firefighters on the scene have so far been unable to find the cause of the blaze, but arson has not yet been ruled out."*

"I hope no one was hurt," said Justin's mom.

"Athlete City is one of the biggest independent sporting goods stores in the country. So far, no casualties have been confirmed at the store where the blaze occurred, but two security guards employed there are still missing," the TV reporter finished.

"That's really bad," Justin said.

"Yes, it is," his mom agreed. "Still — nothing we can do. The police and firefighters are dealing with it."

"Is dinner ready?" he asked, rubbing his stomach hungrily.

His mom nodded. "I'll put it on the table," she said, taking one last glance at the television. "You're not going to Mark's tonight, are you?"

"No. I'm going to my room to listen to music and play on my computer," Justin replied. "Mark lent me a new game."

"Lucky you," said his mom, handing him a large plate of pizza and salad. "Before you go to bed, make sure you put those new sneakers away," she reminded him.

He looked across at them and smiled. The black leather seemed to shine.

"*Of course,* I will," he said, grinning.

Justin dozed happily in bed as he envisioned himself scoring the winning goal in the tri-county play-offs. He would become a school hero! "*Jus-tin. Jus-tin,*" the entire student body roared in his dream.

"*Jus-tin!*"

He turned over.

"*Justin!*"

His eyes snapped open as he realized this was no dream. His name *was* being shouted, but not by hundreds of delighted soccer fans.

It was his mom.

"All right, Mom!" Justin yelled back as he climbed out of bed. "I'm up!"

Justin glanced at the clock on his nightstand and noticed that it was almost eleven in the morning. No wonder his mom was calling. He was late for school!

Moving with remarkable speed considering he was still half-asleep, Justin struggled into a clean shirt and pants and hurtled down the stairs, skidding breathlessly into the living room where his mom was standing, hands firmly on hips.

"Why didn't you wake me up earlier, Mom?" Justin asked, his head getting caught in his shirtsleeve. "I'll probably get a detention for this."

"For what?" his mom asked irritably.

"For being late," he said, eventually losing his balance and tumbling back into an armchair.

His mom stared at him for a moment, and then sighed. "Justin, it's Saturday."

He was about to start complaining about being woken up so early in that case. But then his brain registered the anger in his mom's tone.

She marched over to the living-room window. "Do you know anything about this?" she demanded, pointing out to the front garden.

Justin rose from the chair and went to see. He surveyed the scene with complete bewilderment. Several of the plants at the edges of the largest flower bed had been crushed. Petals floated mournfully on the mild breeze.

"You *know* how much effort I put into the garden," his mom said through gritted teeth. "You've been jumping over the flower beds again, haven't you? I know you do it, Justin. I've seen you!"

"Mom, I didn't touch them," Justin protested.

His mom marched him outside. "Then what are these?" she demanded, pointing to some shoe imprints close to one of the obliterated plants.

The prints were exactly the same shape and size as those of Justin's new sneakers. He was so surprised, he didn't know what to say.

His mom sighed. "I thought you'd be honest enough to tell me if you'd damaged my flowers, Justin," she said, sounding disappointed in him. "This is just not like you. I want this mess cleaned up right now."

"But, Mom —"

"No buts — now, Justin," his mom insisted. "Go upstairs and change into some old clothes — you've got a lot of work to do."

Justin could tell that his mom was close to tears. She was sad as well as angry. It was a lethal combination, and he knew there was no way she was going to listen to him.

He skulked upstairs, walked over to his bed, and reached beneath it for his new sneakers. He hadn't ruined his mom's flower bed — he knew that for a fact. He'd come home from playing soccer, he'd had some dinner, cleaned the new sneakers, and gone to bed. In fact, he'd specifically decided *not* to jump the flower beds!

As he pulled the sneakers out from under the bed, Justin gasped. He felt the hairs at the back of his neck rise and goose bumps appear on his skin.

The black-leather parts and the silver-gray laces of his new sneakers were stained with mud, and soil was smeared on the jagged white stripe that adorned their sides. Worst of all, between the laces on the left sneaker was a single red petal.

No — this can't be right, Justin thought. But his mom would never believe it wasn't him if she saw his sneakers like this.

Justin knew *he* hadn't put on his new sneakers and caused the damage. But, if *he* hadn't, then who had? Could someone have tiptoed into the house while he was sleeping and taken the sneakers? The thought of someone creeping unnoticed into his bedroom was even scarier than his mom's rage.

The more Justin thought about it, the more it

unsettled him. Someone must have come into his room while he was asleep, put on his new sneakers, destroyed his mom's flower beds, and then put the sneakers back.

Justin swallowed hard. Why would anyone want to do that?

"Justin!"

The sound of his name startled him.

"I'm doing the wash," his mom called up the stairs. "If you've got anything that needs to be cleaned, then give it to me now, please."

"Hang on!" he blurted, hurtling from his room and heading into the bathroom, the sneakers still clutched in his hand. He locked the bathroom door behind him.

"Did you hear me, Justin?" his mom persisted.

He heard footsteps on the stairs.

"I said I need your dirty clothes," she said as she continued on up to the landing.

Justin turned on the taps in the sink. "Yeah, I know, Mom, I'll be with you in a minute," he called. He pushed the left sneaker under the faucet and began washing away the mud.

"What are you doing in there?" his mom asked, tapping on the bathroom door. "Are you all right?"

Justin finished cleaning the left sneaker and then frantically started working on the right one. "Nothing, I'm fine!" he shouted back, trying to wipe away mud from the drain. "Just had to run to the bathroom. Must have been that pizza we had last night."

He hastily dried the sneakers with toilet paper, then flushed the soggy sheets away, breathing hard. The sneakers were resting on the sink, the leather gleaming and the laces clean once again.

"I'm not waiting any longer — bring your dirty clothes with you when you come back down," his mom called impatiently. "I'll be in the garden."

Justin stared at the sneakers and then hurried back into his room with them and stuffed them out of sight under his bed. Grabbing his dirty clothes, he made his way down the stairs and dropped them on top of the washing machine on his way out into the back garden, where his mom was waiting.

She nodded in the direction of a broom and rake. "I'll leave you to it," she said, heading off back into the house. "And you can forget about going swimming until that mess is cleaned up."

"Mom . . ." Justin began, but she closed the back door on his protests.

Grumbling to himself, Justin picked up the rake and began smoothing the soil in the flower bed.

"What did you do this time?"

The voice made Justin look up. Peering over the low hedge that separated Justin's garden from the house next door was the gaunt, sour face of Mr. Willis, a man in his late fifties who lived there alone.

Justin sighed. This was the last thing he needed now.

"Have you been causing trouble again?" Mr. Willis continued, looking Justin up and down and shaking his head.

"I didn't do anything, Mr. Willis," Justin told him.

"I heard your mother," Mr. Willis said, watching him. "Why would you want to go and ruin her flower beds?"

"I didn't!" Justin denied hotly, returning to his raking.

"Kids like you have got no respect for anything

these days," Mr. Willis continued. "The only thing you care about is yourselves."

Justin gripped the rake more tightly, trying to shut out the unfair comments. The heat of the morning sun beating down on the back of his neck wasn't helping his mood, and Mr. Willis's unkind words were making things ten times worse. Justin could feel his anger rising with the temperature.

"Bad kids like you need a father to keep them under control," Mr. Willis declared. "Otherwise they just run wild." He paused to look Justin up and down, and then shook his head. "No wonder your father ran off and left you," he added with a loud *tut*.

Justin threw down the rake. Now he was furious. "My dad didn't run off," he snapped, taking a step toward the fence. "He and Mom didn't get along anymore. It happens," he finished through gritted teeth.

Mr. Willis took a step backward. "Don't you touch me!" he exclaimed, raising his hands as if to defend himself. They were flecked with yellow paint. He'd been painting his front door, window frames, and garage door a sickly shade of yellow. "I'll tell your mother you threatened me — you're nothing more than a little thug!" he hissed.

Justin was about to answer back, but then he noticed his mom looking through the living-room window. She jabbed a finger in the direction of the flower bed, as if to remind him of his task.

Justin swallowed hard, picked up the rake, and sucked in a deep breath.

"Thinking of hitting me with that, are you?" Mr. Willis accused, pointing at the rake.

Justin lowered his head for a moment, fighting to gain control of his temper. He remembered a trick his dad had taught him to cope with anger: If someone was getting on your nerves or annoying you, just imagine them with a bag on their head. Paper, plastic, or canvas. Plain or patterned. It didn't matter. He looked up and saw that Mr. Willis was still scowling at him over the fence. Justin stared back, imagining Mr. Willis with a crumpled brown paper bag on his head. A smile found its way onto Justin's face.

"What are you grinning at?" Mr. Willis demanded suspiciously.

"Nothing, Mr. Willis," Justin answered, returning to

his raking. "Nothing at all . . ." His secret made him smile even more.

The ringing of a phone drifted on the warm air, and Mr. Willis turned and disappeared inside his house.

That's it, Justin murmured to himself. *Go and answer your phone. It might be the president telling you when to collect your Nasty Neighbor of the Year Award.* He sighed and continued with his raking.

By the time Justin had cleaned up the mess in the garden and had joined his friends to go swimming, he'd managed to put most of the unpleasant exchange with Mr. Willis out of his mind. They got changed, then hurried out to the pool area, where they dived, laughing, into the water.

They spent more than an hour in the pool, talking in between racing each other up and down. Paul won the breath-holding contest, but Mark managed to beat both of them in their final race.

The three friends climbed out of the water and headed back toward the changing room, but their laughter died abruptly as they entered. The doors to all three of their lockers were wide open. Their sports bags had been pulled out onto the wet, tiled floor and were gaping open, the contents strewn about. Two pairs of sneakers had been flung into the corner.

"Look at my T-shirt!" Mark protested, picking up the sodden, crumpled garment. "My mom'll go ballistic when she sees it. It was a birthday present!"

"It looks like someone's walked on them," Paul muttered, holding up his jeans and inspecting the wet footprints on the material. He stuffed a hand into one of the pockets. "And I had five dollars in there," he groaned. "Someone's taken it."

Justin moved toward his own open locker, his heart thumping hard.

He peered inside.

Though his clothes had also been strewn about, his new sneakers were still in there, side by side. He lifted them up and saw that the soles were wet. There was something stuck to the bottom of the left sneaker. It was a five-dollar bill.

Justin felt as if someone had pumped icy water into his veins.

First the damage to his mom's garden — and now

this. Was someone following him? Putting on his new sneakers and causing trouble so that he would get the blame?

But *why*? Who would *want* to?

Justin tried to think if he had offended or annoyed anyone. But, even if he *had*, would they go as far as this to get back at him?

His mind spinning, Justin grabbed the five-dollar bill and bunched it up in his hand, hoping no one had seen it stuck to his sneaker. Not knowing how to explain how he came to have it, he hurriedly picked up his own jeans from the wet floor and pushed the five-dollar bill into one of the pockets. He'd have to think of a way to smuggle it back to Paul without him knowing.

"Did they damage or take anything of yours, Justin?" Mark wanted to know, still sounding annoyed about his T-shirt.

Justin shook his head and, without looking at his friends, he started picking up the rest of his scattered and damp clothes.

After putting them on, Justin stepped into his

sneakers and bent to fasten them. As he finished tying the laces, he realized that he'd tied them too tight. He reached down again to loosen them.

They wouldn't budge. In fact, it felt as if the laces were *tightening*. He took his hands away and stood up straight, gingerly putting weight on first one and then the other foot. The feeling of tightness seemed to pass.

Justin relaxed a little. It must have been because the laces were wet, he reasoned.

"Lucky they didn't touch your new sneakers, Justin," Mark said as they prepared to leave.

Justin looked down at his gleaming footwear. "Yes," he said quietly. "Lucky."

Monday came around again. Justin decided to wear his old sneakers to school because it had rained on Sunday and he didn't want to get his new ones dirty again.

When he returned home, he noticed that something strange was happening next door. Two police cars were parked outside Mr. Willis's house, their blue lights turning silently. A number of people who lived on the street had ventured out to see what was happening.

Mr. Willis was out there, speaking to a policeman, who was scribbling hastily in his notebook. Another policeman was speaking into a two-way radio.

As Justin stared at his neighbor, Mr. Willis looked up and held his gaze.

Justin looked away — and caught sight of Mr. Willis's old car parked, as always, inside Mr. Willis's garage. Through the open garage doors, Justin saw that the car was covered from hood to trunk with vivid splashes of paint, the same sickly yellow that Mr. Willis had been using. Paint cans lay on the floor of the garage, their contents spilled across the concrete and up the walls.

"Local vandals by the look of it," he heard the policeman say into his radio. "No. It doesn't look like robbery. Nothing taken. Just the paint splashed around. Probably someone with a grudge; someone who doesn't like him. Odd really, looks like they stepped in the paint and then walked all over the car!"

Justin froze as he heard this. Then he hurried past, pushing his bike up the short path to his own front door.

"Hello, sweetie," his mom called from the kitchen as Justin let himself in. "Are the police still out there?"

"Yeah, they are!" he called back as he hurriedly made his way up the stairs.

He pushed open his bedroom door and walked straight over to his bed. He'd left the new sneakers under it. Dropping to his knees, he pulled them out.

There was yellow paint on the soles.

Justin shut his eyes tight; his entire body felt as if it had suddenly been wrapped in a wet blanket.

He stood up and walked over to his closet, then opened the doors and hurled the sneakers inside. Then he slammed the door shut, his breath coming in short gasps.

This is crazy! he thought. *Who . . . what . . . is doing this?*

Justin stood with his back against the closet door. *Why? In case it suddenly flies open and the sneakers come hurtling out?* he asked himself mockingly.

Shaking his head, he went back downstairs to fetch some paint thinner and an old cloth from the garden shed.

As Justin went through the kitchen, he was relieved

to hear his mom was now on the phone in the den. She wouldn't ask any awkward questions.

Justin sat on his bedroom floor, working off the sticky yellow paint from his sneakers with the paint thinner and cloth. The fumes from the paint thinner made his eyes water, and he got up to open a window.

As he worked he contemplated what to do next. *I need to find a way to stop the sneakers from being taken*, he thought. He looked around the room. His closet had a key — and there wasn't a spare. *That's it!* he thought.

When Justin had finished, he placed the sneakers in the bottom of the closet, shut the door firmly, and turned the key. *No one's getting to those*, he said to himself, placing the key in the front pocket of his jeans.

For three days, Justin kept the sneakers locked away until the paint thinner smell had disappeared. When his mom asked him why he wasn't wearing them, he said he was saving them for special occasions. Mark and some of his other friends asked him, too, and he gave them the same excuse.

Justin stopped by Mark's house to return the computer game he'd lent him.

"Where are the wonder sneakers?" Mark asked jokingly. "I'd wear them all the time if they were mine," he said, switching channels on the television in his room. He looked down at Justin's feet again. "Your old ones are hideous."

Justin laughed. "So are yours," he replied.

"Yeah, but I haven't got any new ones to wear!" Mark replied.

Justin nodded, and then took a deep breath. "Mark, this is going to sound stupid," he began. "Ever since I got those sneakers, some really weird things have been happening. I think someone's trying to get me into trouble."

"What do you mean?" Mark asked, a curious look on his face.

"I found the new sneakers with mud on them after my mom's flower bed got trashed. I know I didn't do that," Justin told him. "And you know when we were at the swimming pool? I found that five-dollar bill Paul had stolen from his jeans pocket stuck to the bottom of one of my new shoes."

"But Paul found the money in his jacket pocket later on," Mark replied.

Justin shook his head. "I put it there when he wasn't looking," he confessed. "And that's not all: After that, our neighbor Mr. Willis's car got covered in paint footprints — and I found yellow paint on the soles of my new sneakers!"

Mark whistled. "Maybe it's the person who went into Athlete City after you did," he suggested. "They must be jealous that you got in there before them as the ten thousandth customer." Mark scratched his head thoughtfully. "But that would mean they've been following you around — and would have had to sneak into your house to take the sneakers, and then to put them back, without being noticed — on two separate occasions!"

"I know! It seems impossible — but how else could this have been happening?" Justin said frustratedly.

"I have no idea," Mark replied, shrugging his shoulders.

"Anyway," Justin went on, "I think I may have solved the problem: I've locked the sneakers in my closet, so whoever's —"

"Wait a minute," Mark interrupted, pointing at the television screen. "I recognize that guy!"

Justin turned to see a local news report had just flashed onto the screen. "I do, too! He works — worked — at Athlete City," he told Mark. "I remember seeing him when I got my new sneakers."

Mark turned up the volume. The voice of the newscaster filtered into the room.

"Police are urgently seeking information following a vicious attack on a local man inside his own home," the newscaster announced. *"The man, who is in his thirties, is critically ill in the hospital after sustaining severe injuries. He was repeatedly kicked. A police spokesman said there were no witnesses, and the man seems unable to give a description of his attacker. The alarm was raised when blood-soaked footprints were spotted around the man's front door."*

Justin jumped to his feet, his face pale.

"What's the matter with you?" Mark asked.

"You heard what they said, Mark," Justin gasped. "What if it's the sneakers again?" He turned toward the door. "I've got to go," he told Mark.

"Justin!" Mark called, but Justin was already running out of the room.

He jumped onto his bike and headed out on to the road, pedaling furiously, his mind racing as fast as his legs. If locking the sneakers away hadn't worked, what would? And who would be the next victim?

It was beginning to grow dark as Justin arrived home. His heart was pounding with the effort of cycling so fast, but also with the fear of what he might find there.

There were no lights on in the house.

Justin left his bike lying on the path and paused beside the front door, his hand shaking as he put the key into the lock.

The door swung back on its hinges as he stepped into the hall and reached for the light switch nearby.

"Mom?" he called nervously.

She didn't reply.

He walked in slowly. "Mom!" he called again. This time it was louder and more urgent. Still no one replied.

She should be home, Justin thought, and panic rose inside him.

He turned into the living room, but there was no

sign of her. He moved back into the hall and then on toward the kitchen.

"Mom," Justin said once more, his voice wavering.

The kitchen door was shut, and Justin gritted his teeth as he prepared to open it, terrified of what he might find on the other side.

Slowly, he pushed the door open and felt for the light switch.

The shadows in the kitchen vanished, and Justin immediately spotted a knife lying on the kitchen table. The tip of the blade was stained with red.

Crimson drops decorated the countertop and the floor.

Justin grabbed the edge of the table, feeling dizzy and sick. His skin prickled and it felt as if cold arms were hugging him tightly. Then he heard a noise from above him.

A sharp creaking.

He headed back out into the hall, heart thundering against his ribs. For several long seconds, he stood at the bottom of the stairs looking up into the blackness beyond the landing, wanting to know who was up there, but terrified of what he might find.

"Mom," he called again, wanting so badly to hear her voice. "Mom, is that you up there? Are you all right?"

Silence.

Trying to control his breathing, Justin put his foot on the first step and began to make his way upstairs.

He was halfway up when the hall light flickered for a second and then went out. Justin paused, the fear now a tight fist in his stomach.

It was dark downstairs and up now. But he knew he had to hurry.

Reaching the top, he crossed the landing toward his bedroom. The door was ajar, but not quite enough for him to see inside.

He pushed it open, now barely able to control his escalating fear.

As far as he could see in the half-light, everything in his room looked normal. Until he noticed a crimson trickle leaking out from behind the door of his closet.

His hand shaking, Justin felt in his pocket. The closet key was still there.

He crossed the room and pulled the handle of the closet door. It opened.

The coppery odor of blood filled his nostrils.

Justin looked down to see his new sneakers lying neatly together in the bottom of his closet. The laces were soaked red, the insteps and soles drenched, some of the blood drying darkly around the toes.

Justin felt his stomach contract and he closed his eyes. For a second, he thought he was going to vomit. But after a few deep breaths, he forced himself to open his eyes to examine the lock. It seemed to have been forced open.

From the inside.

For the first time, Justin wondered whether maybe there *hadn't* been anyone following him, taking the sneakers to do terrible things in them so that Justin would get the blame. Maybe the sneakers were doing terrible things all by themselves.

Maybe they were haunted . . . *possessed*. . . .

How else could the happenings be explained?

Justin looked down at the sneakers again.

So much blood.

Whose was it? The man who had been attacked? Whose?

His mom's?

His mind spinning, Justin rushed into his mom's room.

She wasn't there.

Nor in the bathroom.

Justin headed again for the stairs, then froze as he heard the front door open. He listened as the intruder proceeded along the hall, wondering if he would be able to escape and raise the alarm.

"Just what I need! A blown fuse!"

Justin fell against the wall in relief as he heard his mom's voice. And then the hall and stairs were flooded with light.

"That's better!" Justin's mom said.

Justin slammed his bedroom door shut behind him and then ran downstairs into the kitchen.

"Mom!" he gasped, rushing up to her. "Are you all right?"

"Yes, I'm fine," she told him, looking down in surprise at this unexpectedly powerful display of affection. "You'll never believe it. I was chopping some onions and I cut my finger." She held up the finger to show him. "Bled like a pig — and we didn't have any bandages left! So I had to run to the store and buy some."

She frowned. "Are you OK, Justin? You look as if you've seen a ghost."

"I'm all right," he lied. "I got home and you weren't here. I was worried." He managed a weak smile.

"Well, I'm here now," his mom told him. "But I'm afraid dinner's going to be a little late."

"That's OK, Mom. I've got some cleaning up to do in my room," Justin told her. "I . . . er . . . spilled something on the carpet. . . ." He turned and headed back out of the kitchen.

His mom raised her eyebrows in surprise. "*You* are going to do some cleaning up? Are you sure you're all right?" she joked.

Justin tried to smile, but he couldn't. He climbed the stairs slowly toward his room.

He rinsed the blood from the sneakers in the bathroom sink, and then went to wipe up the blood from the bottom of his closet. As he did so, Justin looked down at his red-stained fingers and thought about taking the sneakers to the police.

And what would they say? Would they believe that he

was bringing in evidence for them? No. They'd think he was confessing. Showing them the proof of his crime. They were *his* sneakers after all. *His* sneakers that were covered in blood. What was he going to say to them?

"Excuse me, but these sneakers may have killed someone. I think you'd better arrest them and send them to prison."

Justin knew he had to get rid of the sneakers. He'd never been more certain of anything in his life. He found a plastic bag and jammed the new sneakers inside.

He decided he would take them to the local dump in the morning. He'd throw them as far away as possible and leave them to rot with the rest of the garbage. That would do it.

Justin woke suddenly from a troubled night's sleep. With a heavy heart, he looked over to the bag containing his new sneakers and then swung himself out of bed and pulled back the curtains. The windows were spattered with rain, and trickles of it chased down the glass like tears.

He dressed quickly and put on his old sneakers.

Picking up the bag containing his new ones, Justin made his way downstairs.

He could hear his mom moving around in the kitchen. "Won't be long, Mom!" he yelled.

His mom came rushing out. "Where are you going without any breakfast — and why are you wearing those rotten, smelly old things?" she asked, pointing down at Justin's old sneakers. "Put those nice new ones on and come and eat your breakfast before you go!" she insisted. And then she disappeared back into the kitchen.

Justin sat down on the bottom step of the staircase and opened the plastic bag. Reluctantly, he took the new sneakers out and slipped them on, fastening the laces loosely. He might as well wear them one last time. He'd take his old sneakers with him to the dump and change back into them before chucking the new ones. He'd just have to deal with his mom's complaints when he came home without his new sneakers later.

With his old sneakers in the plastic bag, Justin walked toward the town dump. But he was having difficulty. When he'd played soccer in the new sneakers, they'd seemed to give him speed he'd never possessed before. However, now it was an effort even to raise his foot off the sidewalk. It felt as if someone had lined the sneakers with lead.

Now that he was out of his mom's sight, Justin decided to put on his old sneakers now rather than at the dump. He bent down to undo the new sneakers. Immediately, the laces tightened and the sneakers gripped his feet like an eagle's claws gripping onto prey.

This time there was no denying it.

The sneakers had their own free will.

Feeling icy with fear, Justin realized he had no choice but to fight the sneakers and carry on with his plan to get rid of them.

Wincing with pain, he forced himself to walk, every step an effort.

Normally, it would have taken him less than ten minutes to run from his house to the dump, but there was *nothing* normal about this journey. A few yards farther down, Justin's right foot was suddenly yanked violently to one side, almost causing him to fall over. With a massive effort, he managed to remain on the sidewalk.

The other sneaker plunged forward, once again twisting his torso and making him cry out in pain.

He looked down at the sneakers and gritted his teeth in concentration. "No," he hissed, trying to prevent the movement again. But he may as well have been a marionette, dancing on the strings of some mad puppeteer. He had no control over his limbs.

He winced as pain shot from his right ankle and up his calf. It felt as if someone had grabbed his foot and twisted it savagely. Then he yelled out as his left knee was yanked just as sharply. He gripped the kneecap, fearing that it would burst. Fire burned in his legs as the joints were forced this way and that, twisted into impossible positions by the sneakers.

A man was coming toward him.

"Help me!" Justin called, waving frantically at the man, who just glanced at him as if he were crazy and continued walking.

Justin tried again when a car passed by, but the driver also looked at him, shook his head, and kept driving.

With sweat dripping into his eyes, Justin realized

that he was only a hundred yards or so from the dump now. If he could just keep going . . .

But six lanes of traffic separated him from the end of his journey.

"Come on!" he snarled, glaring down at his feet.

A car hurtled past him. The gust of air ruffled his hair. Justin gasped as he realized how close to the curb he was.

The laces of the sneakers tightened so hard he yelled out in agony, but his shout was drowned by the noise of the traffic speeding back and forth along the wide road. He tried to block out the terrible throbbing pain.

Suddenly, the sneakers seemed to give up the fight.

Justin sucked in a deep breath and ran, darting across the road as quickly as he could. As he got to the middle lane, he stopped dead, his feet jammed to the asphalt.

He felt a wave of pure terror as he looked frantically around and saw a car bearing down on him. The sneakers had taken over again. He was stranded.

He heard its horn blaring and watched the driver gesturing wildly at him to move.

But he couldn't.

At the final moment, the car swerved, missing him by a hair's breadth.

There was another behind it. Then a motorcycle. Both vehicles swept around him.

Justin gritted his teeth and stood still, his heart pounding hard against his ribs.

Keep calm, Justin told himself. *Concentrate. The cars won't hit you. They can see you standing here.*

The police station was on the other side of the road. Perhaps someone inside would hear the sound of blaring horns, see him stuck in the traffic, and come out and help. Justin hoped so. He was prepared to be told off for trying to cross such a busy street, endangering himself and disrupting traffic. He just needed someone to help him.

Again he tried to move when there was a gap in the stream of onrushing vehicles, but it was useless.

Sweat was now pouring down his face. With a huge effort, he forced his feet forward, the traffic still roaring past him on both sides. He moved forward a couple of steps. Another few yards and he'd be on the opposite sidewalk.

The blaring of horns from so many different vehicles

built into a deafening symphony of noise that threatened to burst Justin's eardrums.

Then again, the sneakers stopped Justin in his tracks. A white van swept past him. Justin closed his eyes in terror.

There was a loud blaring to his left — much louder than a car horn.

Justin opened his eyes to see a giant tractor-trailer thundering toward him in the middle lane.

He was rooted to the spot.

The truck driver sounded his horn again, the noise drumming in Justin's ears, the huge, gleaming radiator grille like the bared teeth of a hungry predator.

Justin saw the face of the truck driver, teeth gritted in desperation, as he spun the wheel in a desperate effort to avoid the boy. The truck swung to the left, narrowly missing an oncoming car. The huge front tires shrieked as their rubber burned along the asphalt.

Still, Justin couldn't move.

He looked down at the sneakers with utter desperation.

And then he was hurtled into the air as if yanked by invisible ropes. The breath was torn from his lungs.

He didn't even have the chance to scream as he landed back in the path of the truck.

All he saw was the onrushing mountain of metal, knowing with terrible clarity that, this time, the truck was going to hit him.

At first, all he could see was a bright light.

All he could feel was pain.

The world swam in front of his eyes, and gradually, his mother's face came into focus. Her eyes were red. Streaks of dried tears ran down her face. Justin tried to smile. He wanted to take her hand and tell her not to worry. But it hurt too much to move. And it hurt too much to speak.

There was so much pain.

So he closed his eyes, and surrendered to the darkness.

When he opened his eyes again, his mother was still there. And so were the tracks of tears. A man in a white lab coat stood by her side. A woman with soft hands pressed her palm against his forehead.

Justin groaned. Everything hurt.

"Justin!" his mother cried. "You're awake! Do you know where you are? Do you know who I am?"

Confused, Justin darted his eyes around the room. He was lying on a bed, atop crisp white sheets. A massive stack of machines sat next to him, whirring and beeping. A nest of tubes and wires ran from the machines toward the bed. Toward Justin.

"You're in a hospital, honey," his mom said. "There was an accident. Do you remember?"

A series of images floated lazily into his mind: The traffic streaming by him. The truck bearing down. The world spinning. The sneakers —

Justin gasped, and the machines' beeping suddenly grew louder. The sneakers had tried to kill him!

And they'd almost succeeded.

"Mom?" he gasped. His voice was low and raspy, as if it hadn't been used in a long time. Every word scratched his throat. It felt like he'd swallowed a handful of needles. But he ignored the pain. He had to know.

"What is it, dear?" his mother asked, leaning over him. She grabbed his hand and gave it a tight squeeze. "What do you need?"

"My sneakers . . ." Justin croaked. What if they were in the room somewhere, waiting for everyone to leave? Waiting for him to be alone so they could finish the job. "What happened to my sneakers?"

"Oh, Justin —" His mother's voice broke off into a sob. A flood of tears washed down her face. Justin waited in horror. Had the sneakers already done something else? Had they found a new target?

"Justin, you . . . you don't have to worry about that right now," his mother continued. "I know how you love your soccer, and the doctor promises —" She choked back another sob. "He promises that we'll get you out there on the field again. Someday. But honey . . ." She pressed his hand to her cheek. "It's going to be a long time. And a lot of hard work. Before . . . before things are like they were."

She didn't understand. And Justin couldn't explain. If he told them the truth, they'd think he was crazy. "But what about my sneakers?" he asked again. "Where are they? I have to know."

Justin's mother just bit her lip and didn't say anything.

"When they brought you in, you weren't wearing

any shoes," the doctor explained. "They must have gotten knocked off in the accident." He rubbed a hand across his forehead. "You're a very lucky young man, but your injuries were quite serious, and you need to know what lies ahead of you. . . ."

Justin tuned him out. All he could focus on was his enormous relief. The sneakers were out of his life. No matter what happened, he was safe now, along with everyone he cared about.

"Why are you smiling, honey?" his mother asked. She glanced at the doctor in concern. "Didn't you understand what we just told you?"

"I sure did," Justin said, a new strength surging through him. "And it's the best news I've heard in a long time."

It's lucky that Brian always looked down at the pavement when he walked. Otherwise, he never would have noticed the skidmarks, the shattered bits of glass, and then . . . something even better.

"Hey, Zach — look at these!" he said, calling his friend over.

Lying by the curb was a pair of sneakers. The soles

were virtually unmarked and the tops looked as if they'd been freshly scrubbed.

"Pretty cool," said Brian. "Who'd want to leave them here?"

"Someone must have just thrown them away," Zach said. "They look about your size. Try 'em on. They're just like mine, the ones I got from Athletic City a couple of weeks ago."

Brian took off his old sneakers and slipped on the new ones. "A perfect fit," he said, and smiled.

An Apple
a Day

Tim Barnett was beginning to wonder if a person could melt if the sun was too hot.

He wiped sweat from his face and glanced up at the cloudless blue sky. The sun had been shining since he'd woken that morning. In fact, it had been shining ever since Tim had arrived at his grandmother's farm three days ago — not that he was complaining. He loved the hot weather, and with another nine days to go before his parents came to pick him up, he hoped the sun would continue to shine as brightly as it was shining now.

Tim biked along the narrow dirt track, stopping

occasionally to peer across the fields that stretched away in all directions. The grass and weeds on either side of the track were almost as high as his waist, and the fields beyond were equally overgrown.

He rounded a slight bend, and the farm and its outbuildings came back into view. As well as the farmhouse itself, there was a barn, a milking shed, some stables, a garage where the tractor had been stored, and a couple of rusted pigpens — long since abandoned. Pieces of old farmyard equipment dotted the main yard and the areas nearby like the rusted skeletons of metallic dinosaurs. All untouched since his grandfather's death.

Over the years, during his many visits to Grandma's, Tim had explored the entire farm. The barn in particular had proved to be full of amazing stuff — old farm tools like huge scythes and rusted sickles were propped up everywhere like the abandoned weapons of some strange army. Tim liked the stillness in there and, when the weather got unbearably hot, it was pleasant and cool inside, with its high roof and long, splintered shadows.

The barn was also home to one of the largest spiders he'd ever seen in his life. Its web was high up in the eaves of the barn, but Tim could still make out its eight-legged shape whenever it ventured forth to feast on its latest victim. Its massive webs were all over the barn. Tim had found the remains of flies, wasps, and even other spiders in its silken traps. It was as if the spider was making the barn its own.

Grandpa had died seven years earlier, when Tim was just four; he had only a few memories of him. Dad had tried to persuade Grandma to come and live with them at their home in Boston but she'd said the farm had always been her home and she didn't intend to leave it. Well, what she'd actually said was, "There's a place for everything and everything in its place."

And later, when Tim's dad had tried to tell Grandma that she might not be able to look after the place on her own, she'd smiled, saying, "Don't judge a book by its cover."

That was another one of her sayings. Grandma had a saying for anything and everything and, if he was honest, Tim sometimes found them really irritating.

If he was up a little later than usual in the morning it was, "Early to bed, early to rise, makes you healthy, wealthy, and wise."

If he ate too quickly, he was ". . . eating as if your belly thinks your throat's been cut."

Grandma was superstitious, too. Not just about things like not walking under ladders — Tim knew all about that — but also about strange things he'd never heard of.

One night while they were eating their dinner, he'd reached across the table for the mashed potatoes and knocked over the salt shaker. Right away, Grandma had told him to throw a pinch of salt over his left shoulder.

"Why, Grandma?" he'd asked her, laughing.

"To blind the devil sitting on your shoulder," she'd told him sternly, making sure he completed the strange ritual.

Tim had done as she'd told him, even though it all seemed a little weird at the time, to say the least.

He was startled from his thoughts by a large black crow taking off from a nearby tree. Watching as the bird rose into the cloudless sky, Tim continued biking along one of the many overgrown paths that criss-crossed the farmland like thick brown veins. He had discovered dozens of them during his visits, but he wondered how many more still lay hidden.

Approaching the farmhouse, Tim aimed for a dusty-looking patch of ground. He put down one foot and hit the rear brake, skidding dramatically to a halt. Clouds of dust rose into the dry air.

With a broad grin of satisfaction on his face, Tim looked up to see his grandmother standing in the doorway of the farmhouse, clutching a large glass of lemonade.

"Here's something cold to drink," she said, smiling at him through her large, round glasses, the sun reflecting off her snow-white hair.

"Did you see how fast I was going, Grandma?" Tim asked, gratefully receiving the drink from her and taking a huge gulp.

"Yes, I did. Be careful. You don't want to fall off."

Tim rolled his eyes. "Don't worry, Grandma. Wait until you see what I've got planned for tomorrow," he went on excitedly.

Grandma looked up at the cloudless sky. "Touch wood, the weather stays nice for you," she said.

Tim rolled his eyes again. If he had a dollar for every time he'd heard her say "touch wood" when she was wishing for something, he could afford to buy that new skateboard he wanted.

That evening, the two of them sat watching television together. Banjo, Grandma's beagle, lay on the rug by the old, open fireplace. Tim munched noisily on an apple from the fruit bowl on the coffee table.

"Watch out for the seeds," she told him, chuckling. "You don't want a tree growing in your tummy!"

Tim laughed and took another bite. *Grandma and her crazy sayings*, he thought.

There was a program on about farming in the old days, and how it used to be a big business. Tim watched with interest as the brown-and-white photos and film clips flashed across the screen one after another. "Hey — that's exactly like the one in Grandpa's barn!" he said, pointing at an old plow on the screen.

"You're right," Grandma replied. "Your grandfather used that plow for more than thirty years. Even when new ones came along, he stuck with it. He said that just because it was old, it didn't mean that it was useless."

Suddenly, Grandma turned to Tim and held his hand tightly. "I still miss your grandfather, you know. But God moves in mysterious ways." She relaxed her grip and searched for a tissue to dry her teary eyes. "He must have thought it was your grandfather's time."

Tim gave his grandmother a comforting hug, and then turned back to the TV. But now all he could think about was how little he knew about his grandfather's death. He had been told that Grandpa had been killed in an accident on the farm. No one had ever spoken to him about the actual *details* of how Grandpa had died, but then again, Tim reasoned, he had never really asked. Once, quite a long time ago, Tim had heard his mom and dad talking about it, when they thought that he was asleep. Dad had said that the accident had been unusual. Strange. And all Grandma had said when Tim had asked her about it was, "There are some things you're better off not knowing."

The following morning, Tim was woken by sunlight streaming into his room. He yawned, stretched, and leaped out of bed. As he made his way across the small landing to the bathroom, he could hear Grandma preparing breakfast in the kitchen below. He got washed and dressed, then hurried downstairs.

"Here's a nice bacon-and-egg sandwich for you," his grandmother said.

"Thanks, Grandma!" Eager to make the most of the fine weather, Tim loaded up his sandwich with tomato ketchup and ate quickly, washing it down with a glass of milk. Swallowing the last mouthful, he took his plate and glass over to the sink.

"Hurry along outside," his grandmother said with a smile. "It'd be a shame to miss out on any of this sunshine."

Tim grinned at her. Sometimes she seemed to read his thoughts!

"You know what they say," she called as Tim hurried out and climbed onto his bike. "The early bird catches the worm!"

"Yes, and it's a good thing you touched wood yesterday when you wished for sunshine, Grandma!" he called back.

Tim rode off across the yard. There was a sudden rush of movement ahead of him, and Banjo came hurtling into view, barking and wagging his tail excitedly.

"Come on, you old mutt," he chuckled as the beagle came bounding over to him. Tim turned his bike around and began pedaling as hard as he could, with Banjo sprinting along beside him. The beagle loved having Tim around to play with.

The dirt road was deeply rutted in places, the ground baked hard by long weeks of sunshine. Tim had to grip his handlebars tightly. It was loads of fun — trying to keep his balance over the uneven terrain, while trying to go as fast as he could.

After a couple of hours' biking, Tim arrived back at the farm with an exhausted beagle at his heels. He had a cool drink and a snack, and then looked around for something to occupy the afternoon.

Bingo! he said to himself as he remembered the planks of wood and rusted, old oil drums near the back of the barn. He busied himself heaving the empty old drums into the open and propping up a couple of the planks of wood against them so that they sloped upward like a ramp.

"What are you doing now, Tim?" His grandmother's

voice drifted across to him on a warm breeze as she emerged from the farmhouse, a basketful of laundry under one arm.

"I'm going to jump that," Tim told her, nodding toward the makeshift ramp.

"Look before you leap," his grandmother said, shaking her head as she hung a long white sheet on the line.

Tim puffed out his chest. "I've looked and I'll do it easily," he told her. "I'm a pro at this."

Grandma tutted. "Pride comes before a fall," she answered, bending down to pick up more clothespins.

Tim shook his head, then set off, pedaling frantically. He'd show her — her and her wacky old sayings.

Speeding toward the wooden ramp, Tim braced himself for impact. Nearby, Banjo barked in expectation.

Suddenly, Tim felt something tugging at his ankle. Looking down, he realized with horror that his sock had snagged in the bike's chain. He panicked as the bike hit the base of the ramp. He was losing control.

The bike veered to one side and Tim felt himself falling. He vaguely heard his grandmother shout somewhere behind him just before he hit the ground hard and rolled, his momentum carrying him toward the hedge that separated the farmhouse garden from the yard. He slid into it feet first, thorns digging into his skin and stinging nettles lashing at his hands. The bike cartwheeled through the air and landed loudly close by.

"Tim! Are you all right?" his grandmother cried, putting down the laundry basket and hurrying over.

Tim groaned and attempted to pull himself free, wincing as pieces of thornbush grazed his bare legs and arms.

"I told you to be careful, didn't I?" Grandma said, appearing next to him. Then she shook her head. "You're always in too much of a hurry," she scolded. "More haste, less speed, that's what they say."

"Who are *they*, Grandma?" Tim asked, glaring down at his torn sock and the scraped skin underneath it, and then at his overturned bike. "*They* seem to know everything. Do *they* sit around in a room making these things up just so people can repeat them?" He picked himself up, grabbed his bike, pulled some leaves from his hair, and stalked off in the direction of the barn.

Tim wasn't sure how long he'd been in the rickety, old barn. All he wanted to do was to be on his own in the shade and nurse his injured pride without his grandmother chiding him.

"Dinner in quarter of an hour!" he heard her shout from the farmhouse.

Tim was surprised to hear her call, as he hadn't realized how late it was. *Hmph. Not hungry*, he decided, tearing a piece of straw in two.

His stomach grumbled, and he knew that his body didn't agree with his head. He was, in fact, famished, and it didn't help that there was a delicious smell wafting from the kitchen that he recognized — it was one of Grandma's apple pies. Tim's mouth watered, but he wasn't ready to face her just yet. Though his cuts stung a little bit, it was his pride that had taken the real bashing. He decided to find something else to eat; he didn't know where, but he was determined that he would.

Tim walked to the barn door and peered out. The

sun was sinking slowly on the horizon, and clouds of tiny gnats hung in the air like winged cinders. Leaving his bike resting against the cracked wooden wall, he slipped out of the barn and across the yard.

There was a small copse of trees lined with hedges away to his right and he headed for those. Perhaps he could find some blackberries to stave off his hunger.

As he picked his way through the foliage, he came to a high stone wall ahead. Up until now, most of it had been masked by tall, thickly overgrown brambles that had prevented him from getting close enough to see what was on the other side. But most of those bushes had withered in the heat. Curiosity made him forget his hunger for a moment, as he wondered what lay beyond it.

There were a couple of fallen trees nearby, and Tim hurried toward them. By climbing on the gnarled trunks, he'd be able to see over the wall.

The sight that met his eyes when he reached the top made him gasp. Beyond the wall was a huge orchard. It seemed to stretch away for miles. And every one of the trees in it was laden with ripe and juicy-looking red apples.

Tim prepared to hoist himself up. A quick jump down, grab a couple of the apples, and then out again. Simple.

He knew that the apples weren't his, but whoever owned this orchard had thousands of apples and they wouldn't miss a few, would they?

Tim swung himself up onto the wall, braced himself for a moment, and then dropped onto the soft grass that carpeted the orchard. He got to his feet and looked around him.

This was like no orchard Tim had ever seen. Every tree was pretty much the same height, with the same large split in the trunk that forked into two largish branches that, in turn, split into even smaller branches. Tim was staggered at the amount of apples on each branch. It was a miracle that they didn't break under the weight!

He wandered slowly between the trees, aware that twilight was turning to darkness, but mesmerized by the sight of so much ripe fruit — it all looked so perfect. After a while, he found a piece of fallen branch. He swung it at the lowest limb of the nearest tree, cracking it hard against the wood.

No apples fell.

Tim struck again, and the sound resounded through the orchard like a gunshot.

"Hey, you!"

The shout came from somewhere to his left, piercing the gloom. Tim looked around for its source.

"Get out of my orchard!" the voice roared.

At last, Tim saw where the words were coming from. A figure was moving quickly toward him through the semi-darkness. Tim could just make out that it was a large, white-bearded man, and it looked as though he was carrying a shotgun.

"Get out of here!" the man bellowed.

Tim turned and ran. His fear seemed to give him extra speed but, in the gloom of the twilight, it was difficult to see. He tripped over a fallen branch and went sprawling.

As he rolled over, desperately trying to regain his balance, he saw that the man was drawing nearer, his great white beard like a threatening beacon in the dull, early-evening light. The orchard wall was about twenty feet ahead.

Tim scrambled to his feet, aware that he'd scraped

one knee, but frantic to be out of the reach of this crazy old man.

Fifteen feet.

He continued running, ducking to avoid colliding with a low tree branch, then glancing behind him again.

The man was gaining on him.

Ten.

Tim flung himself at the wall, rough and dusty against his sweaty face. His fingers clawed desperately, trying to find the top, trying with all his strength to lever himself up. He felt himself losing his grip and shouted out in fear as he slipped and fell backward, crashing into the soft grass. He turned to see the figure looming out of the trees.

"I told you to get out of my orchard!" snarled the old man.

Tim took another run at the wall and, this time, managed to get a good grip. He hauled himself up, trying to hook one leg over so that he could drop down safely to the other side, but he realized to his horror that he couldn't move. The toe of one of his old, tattered sneakers was wedged in a gap in the wall.

Below him, the old man slowly raised the shotgun to his shoulder. Tim could see a crooked smile on the face of the white-bearded figure.

"You've been warned, boy," the old man rasped.

Tim tried to pull his foot free. His sneaker remained wedged in the gap.

The old man had the shotgun pressed tightly against his shoulder now, and Tim realized in a heartbeat that he intended to fire.

"You should have stayed away from here," hissed the old man.

With a final despairing effort, Tim wrenched his sneaker free. He slipped over the wall and fell heavily into the copse of trees on the other side, scrambling immediately to his feet.

"If you ever come back here, you'll be sorry!" roared the old man, his voice filling Tim's ears as it rose into the darkening sky.

Gasping for breath, Tim kept running, his heart hammering in his chest, looking over his shoulder, wondering if the man could have followed him over the wall. He didn't stop until he reached Grandma's house.

He crashed through the kitchen door, almost colliding with the old oak table. Red-faced and shaking, he slumped down into one of the chairs.

His grandmother had been waiting for him. "Where have you been?" she asked impatiently. "I said dinner would be ready in fifteen minutes, Tim. Now it's nearly spoiled. And it's your favorite — roast pork and apple pie."

Tim patted his belly and smiled in thanks as Grandma took away his empty plate.

"Are you all right, Tim?" Grandma asked. "You've been quiet ever since you came in. Cat got your tongue?"

"No, I'm fine, Grandma," Tim said, the beating of his heart finally having returned to something like normal. "Just enjoying my dinner, that's all. I didn't want to talk with my mouth full."

"You're right, sweetie. It's just that you looked a little pale when you came in, that was all." She put a slice of apple pie down in front of him.

The pie looked delicious, but the thought of

apples suddenly sent a shiver of fear through Tim. "Er . . . I think I'll skip the pie this time, Grandma," he said.

"But you love apple pie," his grandmother remarked, surprised.

"I know, but I'm not really in the mood for it at the moment," Tim mumbled.

"Well — it's up to you," Grandma said, taking the slice of pie away.

Tim took a sip of his lemonade. "Grandma," he asked sheepishly, "you know that orchard that backs onto your farm — who does it belong to?"

"Keep away from there, Tim!" his grandmother warned, her expression suddenly anxious. "That's owned by old Bill Cole. He's lived there on his own for as long as I can remember. He was there when I came to live on the farm with your grandfather, and that was fifty years ago. Why do you ask?"

"I just wondered," Tim said, deliberately not looking up at her.

"Don't you get curious about that place, Tim. Curiosity killed the cat, you know. And besides, old

Bill Cole hates kids. They're always stealing his apples and he'll do anything to stop them."

Including pointing shotguns at them, Tim thought.

A sudden hammering on the front door startled them both.

"Who can that be at this time?" Grandma said wearily. She made her way out of the kitchen and along the hallway toward the front door.

Tim crept to the kitchen door and peered around it. When Grandma opened the door, he saw a terrifyingly familiar figure standing on the porch.

"Where's that boy?" Bill Cole hissed. "The boy who was in my orchard!"

"I don't know what you're talking about, Mr. Cole," Grandma replied. "And I'll thank you not to talk to me in that tone. Please leave."

"Not until I've done what I came here to do," the old man snapped at her.

Tim stared with a mixture of fear and anger as old Bill Cole loomed in the doorway like a predator. *I have to help Grandma*, he thought. He steeled himself and walked down the hall toward the front door.

Bill Cole's eyes narrowed as he caught sight of Tim.

"That's him! He was trying to steal my apples — just like the rest!"

"If Tim was in your orchard, Mr. Cole, I'm sure he didn't mean any harm," Grandma said. "Now will you *please* leave," she repeated.

Bill Cole moved forward, ignoring Grandma's words.

Though his heart was thumping in fear, Tim moved in front of his grandmother to protect her. "Go AWAY!" he shouted. "Who would want your rotten apples anyway?"

"What did you say, boy?" Bill Cole bellowed furiously.

"Hush, Tim, please," Grandma said quietly, drawing him to her.

Seeing the warning look in his grandmother's eyes, Tim shut up. But he was enraged with Bill Cole for being so rude and threatening to his grandmother.

"I'm sorry if you believe Tim was trying to steal your apples," Grandma went on.

"I'll make *him* sorry if he ever tries it again," Bill Cole sneered. "I don't want people coming near my land, you know that. Your husband knew that, too, didn't he?" A hint of a smile played on Bill Cole's lips.

Tim felt his grandmother begin to tremble.

"But you're on *my* land at the moment," she said back, a tremor in her voice.

"You'd better get that boy under control, or I'll deal with him myself," Bill Cole snarled. "Keep him away from my orchard *and* my apples." He finally turned away.

Tim watched the old man lumber off into the darkness. "Are you all right, Grandma?" he asked, taking her hand and leading her to a chair.

"I'm fine, Tim," she told him, though he noticed that she was shaking ever so slightly. She reached into the pocket at the front of her apron with her free hand and pulled out a little lace handkerchief.

Tim watched as she dabbed quickly at the corners of both eyes. "Somebody should do something about him, Grandma," he said angrily, squeezing her hand more tightly.

"Like what, Tim?" his grandmother said, sighing.

Banjo, sensing Grandma's distress, ambled over and

lay at her feet, glancing up with his big, watery eyes as if to check she was all right.

"Come on," Grandma said, smiling. *"Both* of you." She leaned forward and stroked Banjo. "I'm fine."

"I heard what that man said. I *was* in his orchard, but I didn't steal any of his apples, Grandma. I promise."

"I believe you, Tim," she said, squeezing his hand. "Don't you worry about him. He doesn't scare me. Your grandfather always said he was a nasty piece of work."

Tim stood up and puffed out his chest. "I'm going to go after him and *tell* him I never touched his apples," he muttered. *"And* I'm going to tell him that he was rude for talking to you like he did."

"No, Tim," his grandmother said quickly. "Just let it be. It's over now. I'm fine." She smiled up at him. "Now, why don't you eat your apple pie? I baked it specially for you. And you know what they say: Waste not, want not."

Tim did as he was asked — but by now, he was furious. As he ate, he thought about old Bill Cole. He shouldn't have been mean to Grandma like that — she hadn't done anything. He was just a selfish, old bully, and it was time someone taught him a lesson.

The next morning, Tim was up early and out of the house before he'd even had his breakfast. With Grandma still calling something to him about breakfast being the most important meal of the day, he hurried across to the barn and retrieved a rusted metal bucket, which he hung over his handlebars.

Tim biked as fast as he could toward the copse of trees and the high stone wall that lay beyond.

When he reached the wall, he hurled the bucket over and stood waiting to see if anyone came. When no one did, he scrambled to the top and waited. He heard nothing but the soft singing of birds.

Tim had a good view through the heavily laden apple trees in old Bill Cole's orchard, and he could see that the farmhouse and wooden barn stood about one hundred yards to his left. He hadn't noticed this on his first foray into the orchard.

He dropped down into the orchard out of sight of the house and picked up the rusty bucket. He moved cautiously between the rows of apple trees — he didn't want to bump into Bill Cole.

As Tim drew nearer to the house, he was relieved to discover that the apple trees were planted closely enough for him to approach without being seen. He could hear a soft jingling sound nearby, and he looked more closely to see what was making the noise.

Hanging from the porch of the house and also from the doorway of the barn was a row of old, rusted wind chimes in the shape of large spiders, their metal legs chiming tinnily in the faint breeze. Tim stopped for a moment and watched the swaying shapes before ducking behind one of the trees nearby. He scrabbled around in the long, lush grass, and finally closed his fingers around a largish, flat stone. He then got up, took aim, and threw it at old Bill Cole's house.

It struck the frame of the front door with a harsh crack. Tim waited, then threw another stone. This one hit the door dead center.

Moments later, Bill Cole emerged, looking around, wild anger making his cheeks ruddy. "Who's there?" he roared.

Tim was still ducked down behind the tree, trying not to breathe for fear of getting caught.

After a moment, Bill Cole disappeared back inside his house, and Tim moved nearer to the barn, where he picked up another stone. He threw this one as hard as he could, and again, it hit the front door.

Bill Cole was outside again in an instant, his beady dark eyes scanning the greenery for intruders. "If that's you, boy, you'll be sorry," he called.

Tim held his breath again. He could feel his heart beating through his shirt, and perspiration dotted his forehead.

"I know you can hear me," Bill Cole continued. "Well, your grandmother's not here to protect you now, is she? You heed my warning — don't eat what's not yours. You'll regret it."

The old farmer dipped back inside the house for a moment and reemerged, carrying his shotgun. He strode off across his yard into the rows of apple trees opposite where Tim was hiding.

Tim could hear him muttering irritably to himself as he stalked through the orchard, his voice gradually fading as he moved farther and farther away. Tim waited a moment longer, then jumped and swung on the lowest branch of the tree nearest to him.

Red apples showered down around him, and he worked quickly, gathering up as many as he could and placing them in the rusty bucket. Making sure that the old man wasn't around, he crept over to the next two trees and did the same thing; apples cascaded down, rolling here and there on the soft grassy carpet.

Once the bucket was full, Tim hurried over to the porch of old Bill Cole's house and emptied the apples out onto the cracked wood, then he turned and sprinted back among the apple trees and gathered more apples into his bucket, which he once more deposited onto the old wooden porch.

The spider wind chimes twisted and clanked in the breeze every time he ran past them. Moving as quickly as he could, Tim repeated his movements until the porch of Bill Cole's house was nothing but a sea of red apples. He hurriedly moved apples left and right until he was satisfied with his work. He could still hear the old man shouting far away in the trees.

Tim retreated carefully back across the yard. He smiled to himself; the apples he'd arranged so carefully

on the porch spelled out the word BULLY in large red
letters.

Perfect.

*That's what you get for being so selfish and for shouting at my
grandmother*, he thought.

Tim ran into the nearby barn and looked around.
There was a ladder behind him leading up to a hayloft. He climbed it and settled himself in a shadowy
corner. He knew it was possible that Bill Cole would
come looking in here — but he was confident that the
dark shadows would hide him well.

The view was brilliant. The word BULLY was even
more prominent from Tim's vantage point. From where
he was hiding, he had a good view of the entire orchard
and, even better, of old Bill Cole stomping irritably
back toward the house.

"I know there's someone here," the old man shouted
into the trees. Then his anger turned to surprise as he
saw what Tim had spelled out using the fallen apples.
Tim grinned to himself as he watched from the
hayloft.

"How dare you!" the white-bearded old man roared.

He stepped back but, as he did, he stepped on one of the scattered apples and fell.

Tim watched open-mouthed as Bill Cole pitched backward, the shotgun falling from his grasp. This was better than he could have hoped for!

The gun hit the ground and went off with a thunderous blast. The massive discharge from the weapon hit one of the spider wind chimes on the porch and blasted it to pieces.

Up in the hayloft, Tim was struggling to stay hidden. Inside, he was laughing so much he could feel the tears rolling down his cheeks. He watched old Bill Cole banging his fist on the porch in rage.

"I'll get you!" the old man bellowed. "I'll find you. I know you're the boy from next door!"

The laughter suddenly froze in Tim's throat.

"Aren't you?" Bill Cole continued.

Tim frowned uneasily. But the man couldn't know for sure it was him.

Could he?

"You'll pay for this," Bill Cole raged. "No one makes a fool of me! And no one eats my apples!"

"That's what you think," Tim whispered to himself, and he reached into his bucket and plucked out a large, succulent, red apple. Within seconds, he was down to the core. The little black seeds gleamed at him and his grandmother's words came floating back into his mind.

"Watch out for the seeds — you don't want a tree growing in your tummy!"

Tim shook his head and smiled. A tree would grow out of his stomach if he swallowed the seeds?

"Yeah, right, Grandma," he chuckled.

Outside, he could still hear old Bill Cole ranting and raving. Tim sank back into the straw. He'd shown Bill Cole that he couldn't just bully anyone and get away with it. Then he popped the apple core into his mouth and ate it — seeds and all.

Two days had passed since Tim's daring raid on old Bill Cole's orchard. He lay in bed and let the sunlight stream through the crack in the curtains. It was only eight thirty, and he could tell that it was going to be another cloudless, sunny day.

He smiled to himself. Leaving the rusty bucket

outside the old man's front door, full to the brim with half-eaten fruit, had been a particularly clever idea. He was just sorry he hadn't been able to see old Bill Cole's face when he'd found the bucket. Still, seeing him slip over and shoot the wind chime off the porch had been equally as good. And since then, there hadn't been one sign of the old man coming around to give Grandma a hard time, either — all in all, a great plan, Tim concluded.

He was rudely interrupted from his thoughts by a shudder running through his body, followed by a loud sneeze.

"Once a wish," his grandmother called from downstairs.

Tim got out of bed and stretched.

He sneezed again.

"Twice a kiss," his grandmother added as Tim shook his head and wiped his nose. Was he getting a cold? He coughed. A harsh cough that made his whole body shake. He put a hand to his mouth and coughed again.

It felt as if something was stuck in his throat.

He sat on the edge of his bed for a moment longer and waited for the feeling to pass, and then he got to his feet and wandered into the bathroom.

He ran water into the old porcelain basin and washed his face and hands.

Outside in the yard, Banjo was barking happily. Tim began to think what the two of them could do together that day.

He had just finished brushing his teeth when he felt the urge to cough once more. Tim was beginning to feel a little uneasy. He rubbed his chest and coughed yet again.

This time he felt something at the back of his throat.

Something hard and sharp.

He gripped the edge of the sink so hard that he almost fell over.

He looked into the mirror over the sink and stuck out his tongue, his eyes widening in alarm. There were four small, shiny black objects sitting at the back of his mouth — but they were only apple seeds.

Tim spat them out and looked at them for a second,

then quickly brushed them into the toilet and flushed them away.

He studied his reflection in the bathroom mirror for a moment longer, satisfied that he didn't look sick, and then he returned to his bedroom and dressed before heading down the stairs for breakfast.

"Another lovely morning," his grandmother said as Tim entered the kitchen and sat down. For a moment, he wondered whether he should mention what had just happened upstairs, but then he thought better of it and contented himself by digging into a dish of eggs and bacon.

"Are you feeling all right, Tim? I heard you coughing and sneezing."

"Oh, that was nothing, Grandma," he replied without looking at her.

"Well, I must say, you certainly *look* well. Your cheeks are as red as apples," she chuckled.

Tim put his finger to one cheek and, for a second, he was sure that the flesh there felt waxy and smooth — just like the skin of an apple. Suddenly, he didn't feel so hungry. He shook his head, telling himself to stop thinking such stupid thoughts, and took another mouthful of food.

"What are you going to do today?" Grandma asked.

"Just riding around on my bike and exploring," he told her, getting to his feet.

"Well, don't go wearing out poor old Banjo. He's not as young as he once was. A little like me." She smiled and ruffled Tim's hair as he passed her on his way out into the yard.

"Banjo!" he called, waiting for the beagle to come lolloping over to him.

There was no sign of the dog.

"Come here, boy!" Tim urged, walking across the yard toward the barn.

Silence greeted his calls. No excited barks or delighted yapping disturbed the lazy morning solitude of the old farm. Then Tim noticed a dark shape on the far side of the yard near the barn. "Banjo," he smiled. "Come here. I've been calling you."

Tim walked toward the beagle, a little puzzled to see that the animal was lying on its belly just watching him. Banjo was making no attempt to move toward him. "Are you all right, boy?" Tim asked, wondering if Banjo was hurt.

When he was within a couple feet of Banjo, the dog got to its feet and bared its teeth. As Tim drew nearer, Banjo began to growl deep in his throat, the sound increasing in volume.

Tim stiffened in surprise. "What's wrong, boy?" he said. "It's only me." He extended a hand to the beagle.

Banjo's growl became louder and he began to back away. Tim noticed a surprising anger in the beagle's eyes. The dog barked once, then turned and ran, heading off into the overgrown fields beyond the barn.

Tim stood, puzzled and a little worried by Banjo's behavior. Finally, he climbed onto his bike and rode off across the yard along the dirt track that led away from Grandma's farm.

As the day wore on, the sun reached its highest point in the sky, and Tim decided that enough was enough. He'd been riding around for hours along the endless networks of dirt tracks he always explored, lost in his own thoughts. Sweat was soaking through his T-shirt. He felt a welcome cool breeze blow across him and also became aware for the first time of some slight pain from his calves and ankles.

Tim groaned as he glanced down at them and saw the white marks of stinging nettles. He'd been so wrapped up in his own thoughts he hadn't even felt the plants whipping at his legs.

He stopped, snatched up a nearby dock leaf, and bent down to rub it on the puffy, itching blots on his calves. As the stinging began to go away, Tim dropped the leaf on the ground and straightened up, anxious to find somewhere cool to rest out of the afternoon heat. But, as he raised his head, he felt a little dizzy. A faint ringing had started in his left ear — a sensation a bit like when he'd been listening to really loud music. Tim wondered if he was going to faint. Maybe he hadn't drunk enough water so far — after all, it was a really hot day. Was he getting sunstroke? Warily, he shook his head, and the ringing faded a little. He got tentatively back on his bike and rode on.

As he entered the yard, there was no sign of Banjo. He cycled across to the barn and propped his bike against the door, sighing in relief as he felt the cool air wafting from inside. He walked in — and gasped as he caught sight of the far wall.

From the eaves, all the way down to the ground, the wall looked as if it had been draped in a thin, grayish-white curtain. It was covered with the gossamer strands of a spider's web.

Fascinated, Tim wandered over to examine the web more closely. The holes between the strands in the enormous web were as big as his fist. He was still inspecting the webs when he became aware of movement to the side of him.

Tim nearly tumbled backward in shock as a massive spider hurtled out of the hole closest to him. Without realizing, Tim had leaned too close and brushed against the web.

It was the first time Tim had seen the spider close up. He stared at its swollen, fly-filled abdomen and crawling, hair-covered legs.

The spider began to creep toward the edge of the web. And then, quick as a flash, it dropped to the floor on a thin strand of web and began to scuttle toward Tim.

Unnerved, Tim leaped away and picked up a stone from the floor of the barn, ready to hurl it at the spider. He didn't want to look at it anymore.

"Tim!"

The voice made him turn.

Grandma was standing in the doorway of the barn. "What are you doing?" she wanted to know, seeing the stone clutched in his hand.

"There's a spider in here," he told her. "A huge one."

"There's lots of spiders in here, Tim, and don't you go killing them," his grandmother ordered. "It's bad luck," she went on. "You know what they say: If you want to live and thrive, let a spider run alive."

When Tim looked back, the spider had disappeared back into one of its hiding places. The web was empty again.

Grandma walked over and kissed him on the cheek, and pushed something she'd been holding toward him.

He looked down to see that in his hands was an apple. Tim shuddered.

"Eat that," she told him as she walked back toward

the house. "An apple a day keeps the doctor away, that's what they say."

Grandma left him alone in the barn, and Tim dropped the apple on the ground. He didn't even want it in his pocket, let alone in his stomach. Absentmindedly, he gave his left ear a poke with his finger. An itch had started up deep inside it — the same ear that had been troubling him earlier. The itch remained. Tim shook his head hard, but nothing seemed to help this time. In fact, it seemed to get worse. The itch was joined by a dull rustling noise — like putting his ear to a seashell.

And then it got *much* worse.

It felt like there was a wasp buzzing deep inside Tim's left eardrum — its tiny sting pricking and probing away.

He walked out of the barn, frantically shaking his head and prodding his ear.

Suddenly, Tim became aware that his fingertip was touching something strange in there, bending against his fingertip.

He clamped a hand over the ear, his mind racing,

and rushed over to the house and up to the bathroom to peer at his reflection in the mirror.

Turning his head to the right, Tim stared at his left ear. There was something sticking out of it.

Something green and pointed.

Using a finger and thumb, Tim tried to pull the object out, but it was hard to grip and seemed stuck fast.

Tim suddenly felt afraid.

With his heart thumping hard against his ribs, he tried again. This time he managed to get hold of the object. He began to pull.

With an oozing *pop*, the object came free. Tim stared down at it.

It was a leaf.

He stared at the leaf for what felt like a long time.

A leaf . . . in his ear? How had it gotten there?

Maybe the leaf had fluttered down from a tree as he'd been out riding his bike and landed in his ear. But how could it have gotten in so deep? It just didn't make sense.

As he stared down at the leaf, Tim heard the ringing sound again. And then the itching started again — but this time it was deep inside his right ear.

Something inside the ear moved.

Tim arched his head around to examine his right ear in the mirror — and nearly cried out in fright. A green furled shape was working its way outward — twisting and turning toward the light.

Tim's head was spinning and he felt sick. He waited for a moment and calmed himself down a little before leaving the bathroom and wandering outside for some fresh air. First the seeds, then Banjo's strange reaction to him, then the spider — and now the leaves! So far, this day had been just *too* weird.

By the time he'd eaten his dinner and watched some TV, Tim felt exhausted.

"Perhaps you *are* coming down with something, sweetie," Grandma said, feeling his forehead. "Are you *sure* you feel OK?"

For a moment, he wondered about mentioning the coughed-up seeds and the leaves, but again decided against it. "I'm just really tired, Grandma," he replied. "I think I might go up to bed and read for a while before I go to sleep."

"Good idea," his grandmother agreed. "I'll bring you up some warm milk a little later."

"Thanks, Grandma," Tim said, wearily heading for the stairs. He paused at the bottom. "Have you seen Banjo?"

"He came back for his dinner about an hour ago, but I haven't seen him since," his grandmother replied. "He wouldn't come inside the house for some reason. Silly old dog." She smiled. "He waited until I put his food in his bowl out on the porch before he'd eat it. But he'll be back before it starts getting dark — he likes his basket too much!"

Tim nodded and made his way up the stairs into the bathroom. He was just about to put on his pajama top, when he felt a large lump in the middle of his stomach. He froze for a second, staring down at this horrific pink addition to his body. Tim touched it gently. There was no pain.

He looked more closely and saw the flesh around the lump shining, as if it was being pushed from the inside. He prodded it again. It was as if someone had stuffed a tennis ball beneath his skin.

And then the lump moved.

Tim shouted out loud. He was breathing quickly

now, his mouth was dry, and he could feel acidlike fear rising in the back of his throat.

With shaking fingers, he prodded the lump once more. Again, it moved.

It was beneath his belly button now. Tim had the strange urge to press against the swelling with both hands. For one terrifying moment, he thought that the skin of his stomach was going to split.

His belly button opened like a yawning mouth, spat out a round object, and closed up again. The object rolled across the floor of the bathroom and, as he saw what it was, Tim let out a terrified scream.

Lying on the floor was a large red apple.

Tim backed away from the gleaming red fruit as if it were a bomb about to explode.

"Tim, are you all right?"

He heard his grandmother's voice outside the bathroom door, but his attention was still riveted on the apple that had emerged from his stomach.

"Tim!" she called again, banging on the door.

Tim looked across at the door, catching a glimpse of his reflection in the bathroom mirror as he did so.

There was another lump on his left shoulder.

This one was smaller, but when Tim raised his hand to touch it, the growth swelled beneath his fingers.

Another was pushing against the flesh on one side of his chest.

Again Grandma called to him from the other side of the door.

Tim wanted to call back that he was fine — but he knew that he wasn't. Everything was *far* from fine.

He gripped the edge of the sink as the mirror showed thin tendrils sprouting from his nose and ears.

Like the green shoots of leaves.

"Tim, I want to see if you're all right, sweetie," Grandma insisted, banging on the bathroom door. "Please!"

Tim leaned nearer to the mirror, his face only inches from it. The vision that stared back at him was something from a nightmare.

For a fleeting second, it looked as though the veins in the whites of his eyes had burst. They seemed to swell, spreading across the irises until both eyes turned completely red — as red as the apples in old Bill Cole's orchard.

Feeling lightheaded, Tim blinked hard, and found himself looking back into his own eyes again.

What was happening to him?

He reeled away from the mirror and toward the bathroom door. Only one person would know, he was sure of that. Old Bill Cole.

He pulled his T-shirt back on, his hands shaking. Then, tugging open the bathroom door, he hurried past his grandmother, ignoring her calls, and sprinted downstairs.

He could still hear her calling his name as he dashed out of the front door, but Tim didn't stop. He ran as fast as he could toward the copse of trees, scrambled over the high wall, and landed in the orchard. He didn't feel the thornbushes and the sharp bricks scratching and cutting at his arms and legs.

He ran as fast as he could in the direction of old Bill Cole's house. In his haste, he tripped over a fallen branch and went sprawling, narrowly avoiding a collision with a nearby tree.

Panting, Tim levered himself up on the trunk. At first, he thought his eyes were playing tricks on him, but he realized with terrible dread that they weren't.

On the gnarled bark was a face.

The next tree was the same.

And the next.

Every single apple tree around him bore human features. Etched in bark like the nightmare carvings of some mad sculptor.

Tim stared in terror at them. Some were boys. Some were girls. Some had their mouths open as if screaming for help. Several had bulging eyes, the look of horror in those blank wooden orbs showing their fear and desperation.

His head spinning, Tim tried to stagger on toward the farmhouse, but his legs felt heavy. He rested, panting, against a stooped old tree that was more gnarled than the others, and tried to get rid of the dizziness. But then his mouth dropped open in horror and disbelief.

The face on the tree was his grandfather's.

Tim tried to scream, but he couldn't force the sound out.

He tried again to run, but as he did, he felt something dark and hard tear through the skin of his left forearm. And then his right thigh.

Tim felt no pain, just an awful, grinding, stiffening of his limbs. With a huge effort, he stared wildly down at himself. Jutting from his arms and legs were thick, bark-covered branches.

Suddenly, what looked like a milky-white root burst from his right ankle and burrowed into the earth nearby.

Tim managed to rip his leg forward, but the root flailed around and was joined by others bursting free from his feet.

They rooted Tim to the spot. He tried again to scream for help, but his jaw was now fixed hard. He couldn't turn his head anymore. He felt his entire body go rigid, bark forming where flesh had once been.

He heard footsteps nearby.

The figure of old Bill Cole loomed into view directly in front of him. Tim could see that the old man was smiling, watching as the bark began to cover Tim's face.

DO YOU HAVE WHAT IT TAKES TO BE A MIDNIGHT LIBRARY AUTHOR?

Damien Graves has spent his whole life collecting **"the most spine-chilling stories in existence."** Help him collect even more by sending in a spooky story of your own! In 150 words or less, write your own Midnight Library story, making sure it contains the following items:

AN OLD BICYCLE
A BLOODY SWEATSHIRT
AN OVERDUE LIBRARY BOOK

One Grand Prize Winner

will receive a Midnight Library Classroom Prize Pack!

The Prize Pack includes a **Midnight Library t-shirt**, a **Midnight Library bookmark**, and two upcoming **Midnight Library books** for each student.

DON'T MISS THE SECOND BOOK IN THE SERIES— AVAILABLE NOW!

3 TERRIFYING TALES FROM
THE
MIDNIGHT LIBRARY
BLOOD AND SAND

DAMIEN GRAVES
SCHOLASTIC

NO PURCHASE NECESSARY. Void where prohibited and in Puerto Rico. Open to legal U.S. residents ages 8 to 12. Visit www.scholastic.com/kids/games.htm for details on how to enter and a complete set of contest rules.

SCHOLASTIC
www.scholastic.com

MLC

SCHOLASTIC and associated logos are trademarks and/or registered trademarks of Scholastic Inc.

As Night Falls, a Dark and Deadly Force Comes to Life

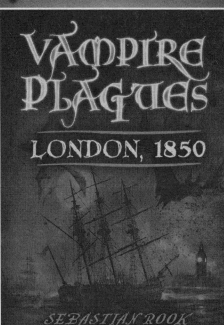

Jack Harkett thinks he is the only one who has witnessed a ghost ship sail into the harbor and release its deadly cargo: a black cloud of bats. Until he meets a boy— the ship's sole survivor—who tells Jack about the vampire plague that killed the ship's crew… and is about to attack London.

VPT